QUARTET EN

MOIRA

Moira is a disturbing and neo-Gothic fable, in which the autobiographical hero in heterosexual disguise plays out his mystico-erotic compulsions. Set in the American South, the novel charts the fate of a university student, Joseph, who murders a girl whom he has raped. In Greek, of course, *moira* is a word meaning fate, and Green's pointed naming of Joseph's victim reveals his customary preoccupation with destiny as it pursues those whose sexuality disturbs them violently, even fatally.

JULIEN GREEN

Julien Green was born in Paris of American parents in 1900. He is bilingual and writes in French. He is the author of many novels and plays, as well as his famous *Journals*, and was elected to the Académie Française in 1971.

JULIEN GREEN

Moira

Translated from the French by
DENISE FOLLIOT
With an Introduction by
STEPHEN PICKLES

QUARTET ENCOUNTERS

Quartet Books   London   New York

Published in Great Britain by
Quartet Books Limited 1988
A member of the Namara Group
27/29 Goodge Street, London W1P 1FD

First published in French by Éditions du Seuil

British Library Cataloguing in Publication Data

Green, Julien, *1900–*
  Moïra.
  I. Title
  843'.912[F]

ISBN 0-7043-0069-9

Reproduced, printed and bound in Great Britain
at The Camelot Press Ltd, Southampton

INTRODUCTION

Julien Green is one of the most gifted bilingual authors of his generation. A prolific writer, he was led by his early experience of isolation to explore the inner world with a natural flair for fantasy. This solitary soil was enriched by the conflicting demands of the spirit and the flesh. In 1914, following his mother's death, Green was converted to Catholicism, but, devout though he was, the complex sensuality of his homosexual nature prompted a substantial lapse in his religious life. Between 1921 and 1939 he lived the bohemian life so favoured by writers in Paris between the wars. He frequently visited Gide, and took up the study of Buddhism and Hebrew. During the war he was exiled to America, returning to Paris in 1945. For many years he has kept a diary, now published as his highly acclaimed *Journals,* and this contains some of his most intensely expressed ideas and beliefs as well as providing an intimate record of one man's spiritual development.

> I would like to be able to tell the truth about myself. I know this is very difficult, that it depends not only on an honest purpose, that a particular form of talent is requisite, and above all, a determination to avoid being ensnared by words. I would like to tell *my* truth one day, one hour, or only for a few minutes. . . . The only means I can see of managing this is to write a novel.

So he writes in 1942, and it is in his autobiographical heroes that we discover the uniqueness of Green's genius. He is able to draw neurotic characters with an irresistible truthfulness which inspires creatures whose manic and anxious existence would otherwise appear to be incredible, even false. In *Moira*, Joseph Day is the triumphant creation of such a masterly talent. A puritanical young student at an American university on the South Atlantic seaboard, he suffers from an appalling sense of isolation nurtured by a religious fervour at once unnatural and naïve. He is obsessed by the sinfulness of sexual yearning, and this sets him apart from everyone he encounters. His preoccupation with hell-fire is accentuated by his emblematic red hair which disturbs the other characters by its very singularity. Moreover, he is unsure of his sexuality even as he is revolted by it. Not only is he drawn to the whorish charms of the local siren, Moira; he is also haunted by the dashing Bruce Praileau, a rich handsome Southerner whose social superiority complements his dark good looks. Joseph's sexual repression is tantalized by their physical beauty. In a momentary encounter with Praileau he notices that

> In spite of the cold his shirt was open at the neck with elaborate carelessness and there was a hint of defiance in the way he straightened his shoulders and threw back his head.

His first meeting with Moira is charged with a furtive longing conjured by a reaction so characteristic of D.H. Lawrence's heroes:

> When he was before her he looked at her, then lowered his eyes in spite of himself.

Joseph's downfall stems from his almost insane obsession with sin, which colours his desires with the violence of lust. Green has written that 'vice begins where beauty ends', but he also observes that

> If one analysed the impression produced by a beautiful body, something approaching religious emotion would be found in it.

Joseph's inability to normalize his response to physical desire leads him to worship Moira's beauty and be damned. Yet because of the novel's careful orchestration of inevitability, his destiny clothes him with a special innocence. He is ignorant of Fate until he asks the benign David to convey his final message to Praileau. Only then does Joseph comprehend the mystery of his relationship with the man whose trivial insult had caused them to fight near the cemetery late at night. The semi-naked Praileau had almost foresuffered Moira's fate during Joseph's rapacious assault, and his instinct prophesies the novel's end:

'You wanted to kill me just now,' he went on. 'You didn't dare, but still there is a murderer in you.'

Moira is a savage fable written with an elemental intensity reminiscent of the Brontës. In probing Joseph's psyche, Green uncovers a dark night of the soul where Eros and Death are doomed to embrace. An entry in his diary for 1944 points the autobiographical aspect of this strange and luminous novel:

Thought today of what D.H. Lawrence said in a sentence that contains all this writer's eccentric violence: 'We are crucified in sex.' Strangely true of many among us. It used to humiliate me to have this problem in my life. I supposed that the great men I admired had not had these difficulties. They simply did not mention them. The sexual question did not fit in with the idea I wanted to form of myself, a somewhat foolishly solemn idea.

Stephen Pickles

MOIRA

PART I

I

FOR some moments they had been standing motionless a
few steps apart and Mrs. Dare was pretending to read the
letter he had just given her, but she had already taken in
its contents and was now surveying the newcomer out
of the corner of her eye. Without quite knowing why,
she felt embarrassed at the idea of looking him in the
face. 'At any rate,' she thought, to reassure herself, 'he
at least looks respectable.'

She was seeing him in profile, his face lit by the sun's
rays sliding into the room between the leaves of the
trees, and in spite of herself she thought him handsome,
although he was red-haired. It disturbed her, that flaming
hair and milk-white skin, and she had to control herself
so that he should not notice that he filled her with a sort
of repulsion. At first she did not see that his eyes were
black. He was tall and rather thin and his dark suit did
not seem to have been made for him. Folding his arms
across his chest he looked out at the street with an air of
defiance.

At his feet was a yellow suitcase, its leather split in
several places and stuffed so full as to look like a ball.
After a moment, changing his position, he stretched his
large hand towards the case, silently moved it a few
inches. Then he straightened up and pushed his hands
into his coat pockets, still looking into the distance.

Possibly he knew he was being watched. He let a
minute or two go by and then risked a sideways glance

at Mrs. Dare, who was still reading. Finally, as though he felt himself justified by his long wait, he looked around him more boldly.

The ceiling was low and the walls were covered with a discoloured, yellowish paper. Near the window two rocking-chairs, face to face, were separated by a little crocheted rug of faded blue and mauve wool. On a round table of painted wood was an enormous plant with strong, glossy leaves; this was the principal ornament of the little drawing-room. In one corner an upright piano displayed on its rack an album of popular songs, whose titles in large print were like a vulgar laugh. The young man turned his head away. 'It's the University,' he thought. 'It's like that at a university.' But at home, in his parents' house, the piano was used only on Sundays. All through the week its keys were protected by a long strip of olive material.

More time passed without any indication that Mrs. Dare had finished reading, for she was still holding the paper in her thin fingers and did not move. 'All the same, I can't send him away because he's red-haired,' she said to herself. She noticed his dusty shoes and concluded that he had walked from the station to save money. She pondered again. 'I wonder if he smells. Red-heads sometimes smell very strong. I couldn't bear that. But I must admit that from here I can't smell anything.'

Suddenly she folded the letter and put it back in its envelope.

"Mr. Day," she said, "do you know what this letter says?"

"Yes," he replied. "I wrote it from my father's dictation."

His voice was rather hollow and was at once hoarse and tender.

"My father is blind," he explained.

Mrs. Dare raised her eyebrows. She was neither young nor old, spare and upright in her grey-and-white flowered dress, her flat cheeks rouged and her black hair scraped back. Her mouth was too large and her nose too pointed for her to be pretty, but the young man decided that she must think she was beautiful to use so much make-up. He did not like her light eyes, which were examining him with effrontery and seemed to pierce his skull. One might almost have thought that the black, malicious pupil, like another smaller eye at the centre of the pale-blue iris, was nailing him to the wall.

"Blind!" she echoed.

And with a sudden impulse she turned on her heel.

"Come with me," she said, "and I will show you your room."

They went upstairs. The boards creaked under their feet and one gave out a noise like the crack of a whip.

Then they were in a light, bare bedroom and the young man looked about him. A work table took up the space between the shallow fireplace and the uncurtained window, and the brass bed, placed at an odd angle, prevented the door from being fully opened. In one corner a cane chair appeared to be in conversation with a rocking-chair which had a piece of wood across its arms to serve as a desk. There was not so much as a scrap of carpet on the floor, where the dark stain was worn away, marking a path from the door to the window, but although the surroundings were so mean they were enriched by the flood of rose-coloured light coming

3

through the trees and tinting the walls and ceiling. The American autumn painted the sycamores bordering the road with all its bold colours from deep violet to red and copper-yellow.

"It's magnificent," murmured the young man, his eyes lost to everything but the gold.

Mrs. Dare let a few seconds pass and then said confidentially:

"The bathroom is at the end of the corridor, on the right."

He was modestly silent and with an awkward gesture put his suitcase down at his feet. Then, not knowing what to do with his arms, he crossed them again.

"I haven't asked you yet where you come from," remarked Mrs. Dare.

He mentioned a little town in a neighbouring State.

"Ah," she said with a half-smile, "in the hills."

"Yes, in the hills."

He pronounced these words in a crisper tone which made the proprietress of the house raise her eyebrows.

"If I remember rightly," she went on, "you're eighteen."

"Eighteen, yes," he replied.

She went to the bed and glanced rapidly at the bed-clothes.

"If you want anything, tell the maid to let me know. There now, Moira has forgotten her cigarette case."

Her long hand picked up a little black metal box from the pillow and opened it.

"You haven't a match, have you?" she asked, putting a cigarette in her mouth.

As though he had been taken by the shoulders he

turned towards her in one movement, his forehead suddenly reddening.

"What's the matter?" asked Mrs. Dare. "You're not going to tell me that where you come from the women don't smoke?"

He did not answer her at once.

"I haven't any matches," he said at last. "I don't smoke."

"And perhaps you don't approve either?"

She was now so close to him that he could see the pores of her skin under the rouge which shocked him, and he noticed, without understanding, that she advanced her head imperceptibly, sniffing the air with open nostrils.

"No," he said, straightening himself.

She burst into a laugh which sounded like a succession of shrieks.

"Young man," she said as she went to the door, "I don't know who taught you in your hills, but you have a lot to learn here."

The boy's face reddened again, but he did not flinch. Soon he heard Mrs. Dare's heels striking the stairs with a kind of arrogance and when she reached the bottom the same laugh as before disturbed the afternoon torpor.

II

LEFT alone he opened his suitcase, took out his clothes, which he hung up in a cupboard, and several tattered books, which he arranged on the mantelpiece. The photograph of his parents went on the table. Not knowing where to put his underclothes he left them in the case and pushed it under the bed.

For the moment everything was going well. He felt calmer, almost happy, and had the idea of writing to his parents to tell them about his journey and describe his room. After looking for a moment at the two faces watching him from their leather frame, he wrote a few lines in pencil at the top of a page, but stopped almost at once. What could he say about his welcome? Perhaps it would be better not to mention Mrs. Dare and her cigarette. His parents would not understand; they would be anxious. And if they knew Mrs. Dare wore rouge . . . He put down his pencil. It annoyed him not to be able to say everything, to have to hide something, for in fact he would be concealing part of the truth. Why had the woman spoken to him like that? And why had she laughed? Admittedly he could have been more friendly, but he had thought her painted face horrible. At home a decent boy would never speak to a woman who made up, and this one was painted like a Jezebel.

Not certain what he ought to do, he left the table and went to the bed, only to come back to the window at once. Not a breath stirred the large gold and purple leaves; the damp, heavy air seemed to cling to the skin. The young man took off his jacket, loosened his tie and opened the top of his shirt. With serious eyes he watched the little street, where an old negro was dragging a cart of water melons and crying his wares in a melancholy voice. 'Perhaps she has crossed my path so that I can save her,' thought Joseph, suddenly.

At that moment someone entered the room through the open door and stood next to him.

"A lot of colour in the picture: the old darkie in his bright blue rags, the big dark green, almost enamelled, fruits and all those fiery colours in the trees. . . . It's the Old South they keep on talking about."

These words, spoken softly, were uttered by a boy of about eighteen or nineteen, plump and swarthy, with curly hair and lively eyes which moved rapidly from one object to another. He added, "I'm your neighbour. There are four of us students in the house. My name is Simon Demuth. What's yours?"

"Joseph Day."

"How do you do, Joe," said Simon Demuth, putting his round damp hand into Joseph Day's large white one. "I saw you just now when you opened the gate. I came in to see your room as the door was open. The two other fellows haven't come yet, but they're expected either tomorrow or tonight. I heard Mrs. Dare talking about it to someone on the telephone."

He stopped to take breath and then went on:

"By the way, I also heard your conversation with her just now . . . oh, quite by accident, the door was open. You know, Joe, that woman's as tough as an old redskin. If I were you . . ."

Joseph stepped back slightly.

"Do you know Mrs. Dare?" he asked.

"Me? No. I only arrived this afternoon. But I'm a pretty good judge. And quite by accident I've found out her age. The date of her birth is written in the big family Bible. Perhaps you noticed it on the little table downstairs?"

"No, I didn't," said Joseph, putting his hands gloomily in his pockets.

Simon looked up at him anxiously.

"You think I talk too much," he said, sadly. "But I can't help it when I meet someone I really like. So you come from the hills, where they sing ballads? I adore ballads."

Joseph made a gesture of impatience and an expression of alarm spread over Simon Demuth's round face.

"Oh, I've annoyed you!" he cried. "It's very odd, but I'm always annoying people."

"No, you haven't annoyed me," said Joseph, at once disarmed.

Simon gave a little skip, like a child.

"We're going to be friendly, I'm sure!" he cried. "I don't come from here, you know. I come from the North. I thought it would be romantic to come and study here. Yes, really! The little Southern town sleeping in its valley, with its white-columned houses, its traditions, its prejudices . . . I don't offend you?"

"Oh, no. I don't come from here, either."

"I forgot. Do you think I have a Northern accent?"

"A slight one, perhaps."

"What a pity. Round here they don't like people from the North. . . . My father is a tailor, but when I've graduated I shall be a painter. Look here."

He pulled a small drawing-book from his pocket, opened it at random and showed several pages. Joseph saw heads of men and women, a bit of a landscape with trees looking like smoke—and hands, a great many hands.

"That's my left hand," Simon explained. "An artist in New York told me I had talent. One day, when I know you better, I'll tell you about him. What do you think of my work?"

Frowning, Joseph thrust his hands into his hair, a gesture which did not go unnoticed. He thought Simon ridiculous and the conversation embarrassed him; he felt ashamed of being with this little man who moved about too much and whose voice sometimes went up surprisingly high.

"I don't know," he said at last. "I don't understand much about it."

At that moment a bell announced that dinner was ready.

III

JOSEPH sat down at the place that Simon showed him as though he were the host. On the white tablecloth were two silver candle-sticks which lent a deceptive appearance of wealth to the poorly furnished room, where the last rays of the setting sun still shone on the skirting-board. An engraving in a black frame over the fireplace only emphasised the bareness of the grey walls, and near the cornice the paper was covered with long, brown stains.

"Very typical," Simon remarked, pointing at the mildew and then at the silver candle-sticks. "You may be dying of hunger, but you don't part with the family relics."

Joseph made no reply. His companion seemed to open his mouth only to make controversial or irritating remarks, and he bit his lips at the thought of having such an exasperating neighbour at every meal. His anxiety not to offend anyone, however, led him sometimes into

9

actions which he afterwards regretted. And from time to time the thought came to him that the people who entered his life were all sent by God. Besides, this evening even Simon's chatter could not spoil his pleasure at being in a strange town, and he looked tolerantly at the gloomy room lit only through a narrow sash window. No doubt when night fell the candles would be lit and, like a child, he made a wish that it would be quite dark before the dessert. At home they ate in the kitchen and the candles were lit only at Christmas, but in the large towns they had their own customs, some good, others not. For example, Mrs. Dare used make-up. This recollection disturbed him. 'I shall help her,' he thought. 'Yes, I shall help her to save herself.' And, filled with a sudden fervour, he saw himself drawing tears of shame from the woman, promises, true repentance, perhaps even a public confession of her faults, as in former times. What a victory it would be!

So vividly did he imagine this scene that he no longer heard what his neighbour was saying and he started when the door opened suddenly. In the twilight he could see the silhouette of a tall young man who came in and sat at the other end of the table, as though he wanted to put as much distance as possible between himself and his table companions. A few minutes passed and a young negress, smelling strong of perspiration, put a plate of soup before the newcomer and lit the candles. This was the moment Joseph had been waiting for. At first there were two little flames, fiery points in the shadow, barely touching the wicks and throwing no light. All at once they lengthened and spread, and everything that could catch the light, their eyes, their hands on the table, the water jug, the maid's white apron, emerged from the darkness.

There was a short silence. Simon uttered a few platitudes designed to show that he was an artist, while the stranger glanced round, letting his eyes slide over Joseph, and bent his head to look at his plate. In his high-coloured face his eyebrows were like two black strokes drawn in charcoal, and as he moved his head a gleaming curve followed the line of his thick, shining hair. This was all Joseph saw, for he imitated the new guest's discretion and fastened his gaze on the engraving above the fireplace. He wanted to say a word of welcome, but although he opened his mouth several times it was no use—to make himself heard he would have had to silence his neighbour. In his heart Joseph longed to make the stranger understand that he and Simon were not friends, that there was no secret between them, as Simon's whisperings might lead him to believe, and that they hardly knew each other, but he could not do this without cruelly wounding Simon's self-esteem. 'It can't be helped,' he said to himself. 'When this boy gets up to leave I shall go and speak to him.' And that moment a voice inside him asked, 'Why?' He was taken aback and could find no answer to this simple question. The stranger, indeed, appeared to prefer to be left alone. He ate quickly, without raising his head, apparently eager to finish and leave the room. As soon as he had swallowed his dessert he rose, gave a half-smile, which might as well have been for Simon as for Joseph, and went out. His footsteps sounded in the hall, then on the porch, and the iron gate closed behind him with a snap like the sound of a pistol.

Simon then answered the question which Joseph was trying not to ask.

"He's from South Carolina. I think his name's Bruce Praileau and he's in his second year. I don't know yet where he lives, but I shall find out. Anyway he's arranged with Mrs. Dare to have his meals here. He looks haughty, doesn't he?"

Joseph hesitated before answering.

"I don't think so," he said at last and, getting up, went into the hall.

Simon ran after him.

"Would you like to go for a walk, Joe? The moonlight will be magnificent on the University lawns."

Joseph, however, did not feel inclined to go for a walk in the moonlight with Simon and he tried to think of an excuse which would not upset the little man, whose mouth was already drooping at the corners with disappointment.

"I must write to my mother. I promised."

Alone in his room he thought, 'You said you were going to write, so write you shall.' He sat down at the table without delay, thought for a moment and began his letter. Moving without haste, his hand covered the page with perfectly even lines. He recorded everything—the journey, the conversation with Mrs. Dare (whose rouged face he described), the talk with Simon, the dinner. Should he also mention Bruce Praileau, he wondered. What possible interest could it have? But it was part of the day like everything else and it pleased him to write the strange-sounding name in the last paragraph of his letter.

When he had finished he opened his Bible and with

his head in his hands read several pages with passionate attention. Half an hour later, having first turned out the light, he undressed and went to bed.

IV

THE next two or three days were passed in comparative idleness. Each student had to register for the courses he had chosen, but there was no question of any work. On the third day after his arrival Joseph was given the name of the professor who, according to University custom, would be his mentor, and went to see him. Mr. Tuck, the mathematics professor, received him in his little office. The window was wreathed with heavy mauve clusters of wistaria and looked out on a chain of wooded hills, whose summit formed a long blue-grey line across the sky. Joseph saw a big, jovial man with unaffected manners sitting in a chair, which he swivelled rapidly from side to side as though to distract attention from the enforced slowness of a fat man.

"Sit down, Mr. Day," he said. "I've read your school report. Your mathematics aren't too good, eh? That's my loss, but it won't stop our being friends. I see you've chosen Greek. You're interested in the classics?"

Joseph blushed.

"I want to read the New Testament in the original," he said, with all the fervour of a confessor of the faith before a Roman prefect.

"Fine," said Mr. Tuck, swinging his chair partly round to face the window and pretending to look at the view in order to let Joseph's colour subside. "But you know," he went on, "they don't study the New Testament now in the Greek class. You'll amuse yourself with Xenophon in your second term and you'll do the Iliad during your second year. After that, if you keep it up, you'll read two of Plato's dialogues in your third year. You're taking ancient history as well, aren't you?"

"Yes."

"Greek, ancient history, American history, English literature and biblical literature. Is that right?"

The young man nodded and could not help smiling, he liked this man so much. He had expected to meet with stiff dignity and cold contempt, instead of which he was being treated as a friend. He regretted his remark about the New Testament, which now sounded rather pretentious, but it was the kind of observation which he often made in spite of himself, as though urged on by an interior force. Mr. Tuck must think him naïve. After a few minutes he went away.

Outside the sun was flooding the long lawns bordered with trees, and students were walking about in a leisurely way. They had all a characteristic nonchalance which the young man tried to copy, for in his eyes everything at the University was right and he wanted to behave like everyone else and to be like the people he mentally called 'the others'. The students called to each other and exchanged jokes. This he could not do, nor would he have dared to, but he smiled at several strangers, who looked at him with surprise. His hair and colouring might have been the reason for this. At home nobody paid any attention to him, but in the train both men and women had stared at him and here, too, he read in almost everyone's eyes that odd expression he knew so well and which was partly irritation, partly surprise. He resolved not to go out without a hat in future and made an effort to think of something else.

From where he was standing he could see the library, its large Doric columns wreathed with honeysuckle, and beyond it a semi-circle of white stone buildings, half-hidden by magnolia trees. He walked at random towards a terrace overlooking a shrubbery. The sunlight, subdued by a fine mist, gilded the gravel paths, and birds with blood-red plumage called from the trees of a long avenue which enclosed the gardens on the town side.

His hands in his pockets, Joseph was watching the traffic passing in the distance when he heard voices behind him. One remark, clearly uttered, came to his ears and made him wince.

"Gentlemen," said a drawling, bantering voice, "does any one of you know the address of the local fire brigade? I guess it would be a wise precaution to notify them."

Joseph did not move. He had heard this obvious joke too often to be surprised by it, but each time it nettled him. Sometimes people just shouted "Fire!" He let a second or two go by in order to master his rising anger, then turned round abruptly. Four elegantly dressed young men were watching him with mocking smiles, but Joseph saw only one of them who stood a little in front, his hand on his hip and his legs apart. It was Bruce Praileau. Joseph took a step towards him.

"Was it you who said that?" he demanded.

Praileau looked first at Joseph's face, then at his shoulders and finally at his feet. Having finished his inspection he replied in icy tones, "No, but I will accept responsibility for it; it pleases me."

Joseph heard these words, which he did not really take in, through a kind of buzzing in his ears. For a moment he could see nothing and the little groups of men in broad sunlight seemed enveloped by shadow. Nobody moved. Finally Praileau's voice rose again as though from a deep pit: "If anyone wants to find me I live at Number 44 in the East Lawn."

'Why does he say that?' thought Joseph. 'If I lifted my hand to him I should kill him.'

He turned sharply on his heel and crossed the garden towards the avenue. Behind him no one uttered a syllable and as he went there was such a silence that he might have been alone, but it was a silence more overwhelming than a burst of laughter.

He walked down the avenue. His feet sank in the dead leaves as though in a turbulent river and for some minutes their loud rustle stopped him thinking. It was only when he was in his room again that he was able to put his thoughts in order. The whole scene came back to his mind with a new and pitiless clarity. Praileau had been wearing a maroon, almost red, suit and his large black tie made an arrogant patch on his white shirt. Why arrogant? Because Praileau's whole person spoke of arrogance. Simon had been right: from head to foot this young man was haughty. His jet-black eyes shone in his ruddy face under strong eyebrows, and he threw back his head like someone used to command. Joseph had seen that in the space of a second and something in him had risen up to oppose this attitude. Then a kind of mist had hidden that aggressive face.

He brooded over his anger all day and shut himself up in his room without any appetite. He tried to read some chapters of the Bible, but the sentences which usually calmed him no longer held his attention. He leant his head on his hands and looked uncomprehendingly at the narrow columns. His lips formed to no purpose the solemn, archaic words. A voice—the voice of Praileau —was louder than his reverent murmur. Hard and calm it repeated incessantly: 'If anyone wants to find me . . . if anyone wants to find me . . .' 'If I'd hit you this morning, I'd have stunned you,' Joseph's thoughts replied. 'I'm twice as strong as you.' Suddenly he said aloud: "Why did you speak to me like that? Why? Why? What harm have I done you?"

With a furious gesture he closed the Bible and stood up so abruptly that his chair fell over. 'I can't eat, or read, or pray,' he thought. 'I behaved as though I were afraid and the Lord hates cowards.'

The door opened and Simon crept into the room with a sharp, ferreting glance.

"What's the matter, Joe? I heard a noise. Why haven't you had any lunch? Are you ill?"

"No. Leave me alone."

"Have you had bad news?"

Joseph shook his head impatiently. Simon caught one of his hands, which was at once snatched away.

"I know what it is!" said the little man, his face shining with stupidity. "Don't deny it, you're in love!"

"Oh, go away!" Joseph cried, pushing him out of the room.

Towards the end of the afternoon the two other students who were to lodge at Mrs. Dare's arrived, just as Simon had said. One, who looked under-sized, poor and studious, and wore steel-rimmed spectacles, announced in an almost inaudible murmur that his name was John Stuart, and disappeared at once into his room. The other, though not much taller or stronger, strutted in and introduced himself with much self-assurance. He was fair, with a large, talkative mouth and laughing grey eyes, and informed everyone in ringing tones that he came from Georgia and that his name was Frank MacAllister. He visited Simon's room and honoured him with a careless dig in the waistcoat and then in the same off-hand way went into the next room, where he was brought to a sudden stop. His laugh froze on his face and he remained motionless just inside the door.

"Come in," Joseph said with a sombre expression.

Recovering his assurance the visitor crossed the room to the table where the young man was sitting. Joseph frowned as the newcomer drew a green silk handkerchief from his sleeve and mopped his face.

"I heard your name just now," Joseph said hurriedly. "You are Frank MacAllister. I am Joseph Day. We are now introduced. Let's go back to work."

"Go back to work!" cried MacAllister. "Wild horses wouldn't drag me! You may as well know that I'm here owing to circumstances outside my control and I mean to drown my sorrows in drink every night. What are you reading? The Holy Bible!"

"You'd better be careful," said Joseph, covering the open book with his hand.

"What's biting you?" MacAllister asked. He raised one finger and intoned in a bass voice: "Six days shalt thou labour and do all thy work, but the seventh day is the Sabbath of the Lord thy God."

18

Joseph jumped up. "Mr. MacAllister," he cried, "this room has two exits—the door and the window. Which would you prefer?"

"Oh, you don't scare me," said MacAllister, flicking his handkerchief defiantly. "If you want a fight, you know, we'll have one."

He stood firm, his hands on his hips.

"My friend," said Joseph, suddenly gentle, "allow me to show you out."

Going up to MacAllister he wrapped one arm round him, lifted him off the ground and carried him to the landing, where he dropped him. Back in his room he shut the door and turned the key. Silence fell on the house and then after several minutes he heard MacAllister declaiming Shakespeare at the top of his voice in Simon's room. "Friends, Romans, countrymen, lend me your ears. I come to bury Cæsar . . ."

'At least he tried to stand up to me,' Joseph thought.

That evening at dinner he hardly said a word, in spite of the efforts of Simon, who talked to him in a low voice, occasionally nudging him. The places were all filled and the little room was loud with the murmur of voices. John Stuart sat shyly at the end of the table, where Bruce Praileau had dined the night before. The wretched little man was constantly lowering his head, as every time he raised his eyes he met Joseph's gaze and found it unendurable.

Of the four newcomers one was obviously from the country. Tall, thin and red-faced, with long strands of hair falling over his eyes, he grasped his fork in an enormous fist and when he thought no one was looking picked up his meat furtively with his fingers. Simon was wondering by what misapprehension he had strayed into a university and whispered in Joseph's ear that he was going to make it his business to find out.

"You'll notice," he said with a note of annoyance, "that Bruce Praileau has not come back. This place is no doubt too modest for a young man of such good family."

"Of such good family . . ." repeated Joseph, whose head swam at the mere mention of Praileau's name.

"One of those families dying of hunger in their ancestral homes. They make me mad, these Southerners with their pretensions and their silver," he added in a lower tone. "Don't they annoy you sometimes?"

Joseph did not reply, but he looked at John Stuart, whose eyes wavered behind his glasses.

Meanwhile, since the meal started MacAllister had been holding forth with extravagant gestures, and although as he spoke he turned to his neighbours on either side his discourse was addressed to someone he did not name and who could only have been Joseph.

"Ben," he said to a big, placid youth whose healthy cheeks were covered with yellow down, "if you had to fight a duel what weapon would you choose? You'd choose a sword to hack your adversary's face in pieces and to thrust into his breast so that the point pierced his heart, if he had one."

Ben opened his mouth and filled it avidly with peas. Turning to his left-hand neighbour, who was head and shoulders taller than himself, MacAllister looked up at him and exclaimed: "You would use a revolver. There would be no unpleasant bloodshed. Just a hole in the head, one morning at dawn. Eh, George? That would teach him, the brute. *Sic semper tyrannis!*"

"Don't get excited," said George, pouring himself some water.

He had a flat, sallow face and a small straight nose covered with freckles. He opened his thin lips again and said: "Where I come from we settle our differences with our fists."

He had scarcely finished speaking when Joseph folded his napkin and left the dining-room. On the porch he took a deep breath. The air was cooler now, but still smelt of dust, and across the road the white pillars of the houses shone in the dusk. He went down to the road and took a few steps. He had suddenly felt unwell in the dining-room, but now he was better. With assumed ease he thrust his hands in his pockets and began to whistle a tune he had heard on the way from the station. Nearly all the students walked with their hands in their pockets and he wanted to be like them. Then he stopped whistling and, taking a piece of paper from his pocket, examined it under a street lamp. It was a plan of the University which had been given to him in the secretary's office.

It was impossible to lose the way. The road curved round the gardens like a long arm and on reaching the library one left it and crossed to the great lawn with arcades on either side. That was the place. He put the plan back in his pocket and quickening his step walked to the end of the road, then turned right and crossed the avenue.

He noticed an opening in the low wall running round the garden which led to a brick path mounting obliquely to the library. He hesitated to take it, thinking vaguely that it might be forbidden, but, reassured by the solitude, he got over the wall and plunged under the trees. At this hour there was no one about. Most of the students were still having dinner, and those who had finished had gone into the town. Joseph walked towards the library. Its tall marble pillars were outlined against the black sky, but all at once the trees hid it from view. He went on, then left the path, to climb some steps leading to a covered walk. He thought of going back; perhaps he should have followed the plan rather than take a short cut, but after a moment's reflection he turned left, skirted a brick wall and went up some more steps.

V

Much to his surprise he had reached the place he had looked for on the plan. He strained his eyes down the two arcades running on either side of the long lawn like the pavements of a grass road. The white columns supporting the arches of the arcades seemed to draw closer together as they receded so that at the far end they closed up to form a barrier. The effect was of a cloister. Two rows of dark green doors stood out almost black against the pale pink brick, and on each door was a number in brass figures and a visiting card.

Joseph had already learned from Simon that these rooms looking on to the great lawn were let to students who sometimes booked them several years ahead. They were greatly prized and it gave a certain prestige to be able to say: 'I live at such-and-such a number in the East, or West, Lawn.' He instinctively took his hands out of his pockets and walked quietly to Number 44. The visiting card showed that he had made no mistake, and, without knowing why, he blushed slightly on reading the name. He had heard Simon pronounce it and had written it himself in his letter to his mother, but to see his enemy's name engraved in fine capital letters on the white card disturbed him. 'What arrogance!' he thought. And he repeated this phrase to himself several times. After a moment's hesitation he knocked loudly on the door.

There was no reply at first. Then a door near-by opened and a young man in shirt-sleeves appeared on the threshold in a large rectangle of yellow light.

"Praileau's not in," he said.

"When will he be back?" Joseph asked.

He was answered by a shrug of the shoulders. The door closed again and Joseph heard a guitar being tuned.

What was he to do? Leaving the arcade he wandered about the lawn and then sat down on the grass, his hands holding his knees, looking up at the stars. They shone brilliantly against the black sky; some of them quivered. From a childhood habit he looked for the Great Bear; he had once been told that his birthplace was just underneath it. He lay down on his back and the sky became a vast river bearing thousands of lights on its waters. He picked a stem of grass and chewed it. Turning his head towards Bruce Praileau's door he thought: 'I shall wait for him all night, if need be.'

All night. Did he hate him, then? It was not an easy question. He did not hate him; he wanted to fight him. In spite of everything he had to smile at this way of looking at it. He forgave Praileau his insolence, forgave him sincerely. If he did not forgive him what was the use of reading the Gospels? But every now and then a wave of anger broke over him. To admonish the wicked, to strike them for their own good, if necessary, seemed his duty. One could be angry and not sin. The Gospel said: "Whoever is angry with his brother without a cause . . ." Suddenly he fell asleep.

He was woken up by some students crossing the lawn singing. One of them passed quite near him without noticing and almost tripped over his prostrate body, for he was drunk and made his way with his hands out, as though feeling for some invisible support. Disgusted, Joseph watched the unsteady figure move away in the shadows, then jumped up and crossed to the arcade. A thin line of light came from under the door and he could hear someone in the room singing quietly.

'What shall I say to him?' Joseph asked himself. He suddenly noticed that sweat was running down his forehead and he wiped it off with the back of his hand before knocking at the door with his closed fist. The song stopped short and the door opened almost at once.

"Oh, it's you," Praileau said. "Come in."

It was a rather small room with a large window divided into little panes, and a brick fireplace surmounted by a painted wooden mantelpiece. The blankets on the iron bed had been thrown back in a heap, a sheet being enough covering on such a warm night. The inevitable rocking-chair, a second chair and a little work table made up the furniture in this austere room, reminiscent of a monastic or prison cell, which had been occupied by five generations of students.

24

"I was wondering if you'd come," Praileau remarked. "I thought probably not."

He had taken off his jacket and his white shirt brought out the warm colouring of his skin, half-way between red and brown. His black silk tie somehow counteracted any carelessness in his dress. Joseph fixed his eyes on this tie, not wanting to look higher, for the calm, superior face made him furious.

"Well?" Praileau said after a few seconds.

With a sudden movement Joseph clutched the black tie.

"I didn't like what you said to me this morning," he muttered in a stifled voice.

"Right," replied Praileau, "but let go of me. We can't fight here."

Joseph let his hand fall.

With complete calm Praileau loosened his tie slightly and put on his coat, which was thrown over the back of a chair. No trace of anger appeared on his face; rather a faint weariness. Joseph could not help admiring a self-control which contrasted so strongly with his own agitation.

But when they had left the room and Praileau was about to double-lock the door Joseph saw him fumbling so awkwardly with his key that he drew nearer to watch. To his stupefaction he saw Praileau's hand shaking violently. In an instinctive movement of shame he moved away, as though he had seen something he should not.

"We'll go over to the cemetery," Praileau said, putting the key in his pocket. "There's a place I know, near where the Dean of Medicine lives, where we won't be disturbed."

They crossed the lawn, skirting the west arcade, and went down a slope to the shrubbery. Praileau walked with deliberation and Joseph matched his steps, but neither spoke until they were in the open. They had passed the Dean's house with its frail white pillars, which could just be seen standing back from the road, when Praileau spoke.

"You know my name because you read it on my door, but I don't know yours."

"Joseph Day."

There was a silence. Their feet made a muffled noise on the dusty road. The frogs in the hollows of the trees uttered small, clear, tremulous sounds. Joseph took advantage of the darkness to look at his companion. He tried to see his face, but could distinguish only his forehead framed by black hair and two points of light shining in the hollows of his eyes. Once or twice he felt like striking that proud head and punishing it for what it had said and for all it was secretly thinking. Then this inner violence gave way to a sudden, intoxicating gentleness, a strange longing to love all creatures—a longing which he confused with the promptings of religion. With what joy he could forgive the man walking beside him the insult of the morning! In a moment he would have seized his hand without further explanation. But Praileau would not have understood; he would think the gesture came from fear. What contemptuous words would rise to his lips! At this thought Joseph again felt the rush of anger which so often blinded him.

"Here we are," Praileau said, stopping. "The wall you can see is the cemetery wall. Behind us is the pond where the boys come and bathe. We shall be quiet here."

They left the path and walked a little way on the grass under the trees.

"Take off your coat," said Praileau. "I shall see you better."

He took off his own coat and threw it on the ground. Joseph obeyed him with fury. It was Praileau's voice which put him beside himself; its intonations seemed to say: 'I am better than you.' Even Praileau's accent betrayed his background, of which he was doubtless proud. And as for the careless way he gave orders . . .

Joseph suddenly threw himself on Praileau. He was moved by something irresistible, a blind force urging him on. The shock made Praileau lose his balance and he fell to the ground dragging his opponent with him. For several minutes they rolled and struggled together, panting in the dark like two wild animals, but Joseph was heavier and somewhat taller and got the upper hand. A sudden, mad joy filled him at his own strength and he felt some mysterious hunger in him being satisfied. His enemy twisted vainly in his grip; Joseph held him between his legs as in a vice and twice made his shoulders touch the ground. Praileau was motionless now and gasping. Joseph took his head between his hands and cried in a hoarse voice, broken by his efforts: "If I liked I could smash your head like an eggshell!"

The answer came in a whisper.

"You wouldn't dare. You're scared."

In the short silence which followed Joseph heard the sound of their breathing, and around them the noise of the tree-frogs filling the air with an uninterrupted liquid note, and the two sounds were curiously blended. He tried to laugh.

27

"What should I be scared of?"

"If you weren't scared," the loser's voice answered more slowly, "you wouldn't have attacked me by surprise. You're afraid of me."

"That's not true."

"I shan't believe that unless you fight according to the rules."

At these words Joseph suddenly let go of Praileau's head and his shaking, hesitant hands went round the other's neck.

"No!" Praileau shouted. "You'll hang!"

With an abrupt wrench he brought his opponent down and freeing one arm struck him across the face with the palm of his hand.

"Get up!" he ordered.

Joseph let go and stood up dizzily, while Praileau, hardly on his feet, jumped back. He tore off his shirt, which was clinging to his skin and his body glistened with sweat. Joseph instinctively turned away his eyes.

"I should take yours off too," Praileau said.

"No," Joseph muttered.

"Just as you like. You made my shoulders touch the ground. Now I am going to lay you out at my feet, but my methods will be different. Are you ready?"

Joseph put himself on guard and took a step forward. Immediately a well-aimed blow took him on the chin and sent him sprawling on the grass. He was so surprised that he did not move. Praileau said calmly: "I can do that again if you like."

His words reached Joseph through a mist and he felt that he had just woken from a nightmare. Gathering his strength, he rose to his knees and then stood up.

"Right," he said. "Now we're quits. Let's shake hands."

"You had better hear what I'm going to say first," Praileau answered. "Then you'll see whether you still want to shake hands. You must have noticed that I don't eat at Mrs. Dare's any more."

"Yes, I had noticed."

"That's on your account."

"But why?" Joseph asked.

"You'll know some day, perhaps. In any case I don't want to see you again and if we do happen to meet we shan't speak to each other."

"What have you against me?"

"Nothing. But that's not all."

He picked up his shirt and began slowly to dry his arms and chest.

"Yes, there's something else," he said in a quiet voice. "You're a murderer."

"What's that you say?" Joseph growled, moving towards him.

Praileau did not budge, but the hand holding his shirt was motionless on his chest.

"You wanted to kill me just now," he went on. "You didn't dare, but still there is a murderer in you."

Not a sound came from Joseph. He was so close to Bruce Praileau that he could feel the heat of his body, but he did not move.

The drawling voice went on: "Do you still want to shake hands, Joseph Day? It's now or never."

"I don't know," Joseph murmured.

"Then it's never," said Praileau, with a note of regret. "Perhaps it's for the best; we should certainly never have

29

spoken to each other again. I'm going to stay here and bathe in the pond."

For a second or two Joseph appeared to be about to speak; his hand hesitated, then he changed his mind. Praileau moved away and when he was under the trees unbuttoned his trousers and let them fall. Joseph turned away abruptly and looked at the path. Then he whipped round and called into the darkness, "I forgive you everything you've said, Praileau!"

A loud, mocking laugh answered him from the distance.

"You're a big fool, Joseph Day! Nobody wants your forgiveness."

And at the same moment Joseph heard the sound of a body plunging into the water and then the muffled noise of swimming. Something forced him to listen to this calm, gentle sound which was soon lost in the loud, crystalline murmur of the tree-toads. With an effort he walked away.

As he was passing a little wood he left the path and walked under the trees, his hands stretched out to part the branches. At his feet last summer's dry leaves rustled like water and the bitter smell of decaying vegetation rose to his nostrils. His eyes became accustomed to the thicker shadows and in a semi-circular clearing he stood still.

Among the trees he felt far from the University, from Bruce Praileau, from everything; nobody even knew he was there. Suddenly he began to scream. He could not help himself. He was shaken with a terrible rage; trembling, he took a step forward in the darkness and stumbled against a large fallen branch. He picked it up and tried to break it, but it was too tough. In vain he bent it across his knee, using both arms. Then brandishing it like a club he went forward striking at the trunk of a tree which gave out a hollow sound. It was a young sycamore. Joseph struck it again and the leaves shivered slightly; after another, harder blow the young man felt a leaf brush his cheek like a hand. His arms seemed to act of their own accord, as though they did not belong to him, rising and falling in great slanting gestures and he could hear the whistling of the branch through the air.

For several minutes he slashed at the sycamore with all his strength, his feet planted in the soft earth, his head thrown back. Suddenly he became giddy, went back a few paces, turned round on himself like a drunken man and fell over backwards, still clutching the branch. As he dropped it, it hit his forehead and he gave a little cry of pain, but almost at once he fell into a heavy sleep.

VI

HE got back shortly after midnight. A light was shining in the hall as he opened the front door and Mrs. Dare, still fully dressed, approached him with a cigarette in her hand.

"I'll let you have a key," she said quietly. "Tonight I left the door open for you."

She looked at him coolly, blinking through the cigarette smoke.

"You've hurt yourself," she added in the same tone. "There's blood on your hair."

"I know," Joseph replied.

Throwing back her head, she drew on her cigarette.

"A fight, I suppose?"

He hesitated, then replied: "As you say, I've been fighting."

'Naturally,' she thought, 'with that red hair. . . .'

"I hope you haven't stayed up so late on my account."

Mrs. Dare smiled at his simplicity.

"No. I never go to bed before one. In any case I shouldn't have missed my sleep just for you. I was writing a letter."

She fell silent. Joseph noticed that her make-up seemed redder and more artificial under the electric light than by day. In spite of this she made a better impression and her manner seemed softened.

"Good-night, ma'am," he said, with one foot on the stairs.

Slightly surprised, Mrs. Dare raised her eyebrows; no doubt she wanted to continue the conversation, but he did not consider it was a suitable time and went straight up to his room.

When she had locked the front door Mrs. Dare went back to her room, which she looked at with some impatience. A small, pink-shaded lamp lit one corner of the room, leaving the other three-quarters in shadow. Just visible were the sheets and blankets thrown back over the brass bed-rail and a rocking-chair with pale green cushions. An electric fan on the dressing-table filled the silence with a rhythmic murmur and at regular intervals a corner of the muslin curtain stirred in the cool breeze. From time to time moths struck the mosquito-netting at the open window with a dull sound.

For several minutes Mrs. Dare listened to the footsteps going to and fro in the room above—Joseph's room. Was he never going to bed? She waited, then, sitting down at the table, went on with her letter:

"I hope this fresh anxiety you are causing me will be the last. If not, you will just have to get used to getting on without me in the future."

She crushed her cigarette in the ash-tray and went on:

"You have never been a consolation to me. Your wicked disposition has been my cross for fifteen years. I brought you up like my own daughter and you had everything you wanted, but you have never wanted to admit that I made any sacrifices for you. I spent what remained of my youth in worry and poverty so that you could have a decent education. You resented that. You resent everything. You defied me. At heart you hate me. You broke the big mirror in my bedroom on purpose. It was you who stole my ruby brooch. All your instincts are bad. To crown everything you are common. I am ashamed of you. When you were only a little girl I knew you would never be a lady. You come from heaven knows where. I advise you not to let anyone get a good look at your hands—they would give you away. Particularly your nails. I have my own theory about that. Your behaviour with the Armstrong boy is unspeakable. If you imagine I didn't hear you on the porch . . . If you imagine . . ."

Suddenly, with a shrug, she threw down her pen and tore up the letter. Writing these words relieved her a little, like screaming or weeping, but she could not possibly send a letter like that. For one thing, she did not want to appear to be complaining. Moira was like most other girls. The young generation was worthless, everyone said so. No doubt it was the fault of the war. Things went on now at the University which in the old days no one would have thought possible.

She became absorbed in watching the fan. The blades turned slowly on their axis, first to the right then, after a second's pause and at the same speed, to the left. After watching for some time Mrs. Dare began to feel the fan was human. It looked like a large black eye vainly searching for someone on all sides—no one on the right, no one on the left. Now its buzzing sounded like annoyance, now like grief.

Dragging her thoughts away, she took up her pen again and angrily wrote several lines in a firm, upright hand:

"Of course, my angel, send me the bill, but mind it's the last. The headmistress wrote that you were not working very hard. No one can force you to study if you don't want to, but you will be sorry later. And another thing, you drink too much. Don't deny it, I know it's true. At your age I drank one julep on Sunday mornings and two or three wretched cocktails during the week. My father used to slap me, not on account of the julep, which he mixed himself (crushing the mint first, of course, it's crazy to make it any other way), he slapped me when I smelt of gin. I used to drink a whole jug of water and run about outside with my mouth open after each cocktail, but I couldn't deceive him. He made me shout 'Halt!' in his face and if I smelt of gin—a slap. But I'm drivelling. Write to me if you really want anything. Yours, Mary Dare."

She added a sentence, rapidly, as though all in one breath:

"P.S. You can't come home before the Christmas holidays because a red-haired student has your room."

A red-haired student—how odd that sounded! She appeared to be saying that if only the student's hair had been another colour Moira could have come home. However, she had written it now and she was not going to cross it out.

"What's it matter?" she said, addressing the envelope.

She took off her clothes, her dark blue dress sliding over her thin body with a noise like a sigh.

"Fool!" she cried suddenly, without indicating for whom she meant this insult.

She took off her vest. Her flat breasts and full stomach were reflected in the mirror on the dressing-table. She rumpled her hair with both hands as though to shut out the sight.

She knelt down, bowed over the foot of the bed, her head rolling from side to side on the white sheet in an unintelligible murmur of prayers. After some time she rose, slid nimbly into bed like a little girl and, stretching out her long, thin arm, turned off the light. Outside the frogs were croaking in the trees and in the dark their continuous cry seemed to become more intense.

Upstairs the footsteps had stopped. The red-haired student had presumably gone to bed. By a coincidence of which she had only just become aware their beds were in exactly the same position, one over the other. If her eyes could have pierced both the shadows and the ceiling she could have seen him asleep, seen his large, milk-white body.

'Go to sleep, you old fool,' she thought.

But she could not sleep.

VII

CLASSES began the next day. At a quarter to eight Joseph was the first to arrive in a large room with windows open to the country. Beyond the woods surrounding the town could be seen a long range of smoky-blue hills. As he glanced in their direction it occurred to the young man that to reach his home he would only have to go on walking in that direction, but he did not dwell on this thought. He was glad to be in this room lined with books. He had never seen so many, and above the white wooden shelves hung black-framed engravings of old ruined towns, a triumphal arch gnawed by time, and three columns in a desert. Between these walls was an atmosphere of work and serious study. Merely to look around him made him eager to learn.

He drew near the books and read a title at random: *Titi Livii Ab Urbe Condita Libri I—X*, and recoiled frightened, as though someone had asked him what that meant. Where he was standing he could smell the honeysuckle framing one of the windows and he smiled with pleasure at the strong, sweet scent. But he no longer felt as carefree as on his first day; a hidden uneasiness set him pacing round the large table, and he wondered if eight o'clock would ever strike. A big lexicon lay open on the table and near it some papers left by a student. He turned back to the shelves looking for the Bible, but could see only titles he did not understand.

A voice near him said: "Perhaps I can help you. I know this library a little."

Joseph turned round and saw a young man with well-brushed black hair. This was the first thing that struck him, and then he noticed the deep blue eyes under thick eyebrows.

"My name is David Laud," said the newcomer, shaking Joseph's hand.

Joseph gave his name, not without a moment's hesitation.

"Joseph," David Laud said with a smile that showed very white teeth. "Call me David."

He was a little shorter than Joseph, but with broader shoulders. He held himself like a soldier and returned Joseph's gaze without wavering. There was something bold and questioning in his deep blue eyes which put Joseph on his guard.

"Will you be my friend?" David asked suddenly.

"Sure!" Joseph said.

When anyone spoke to him like that his defences vanished: he was always ready to love.

"What book were you looking for?"

Joseph hesitated again, not sure what the other would think of him. Then he was ashamed of his weakness.

"The Holy Bible," he replied firmly.

"You'll only find it here in Latin or Greek. All the books in this library are in one or the other."

Eight o'clock began to strike as David Laud was speaking and five or six more students came in. Among them was Simon Demuth, who hurried over to Joseph.

"I waited for you at Mrs. Dare's," he said in a reproachful voice. "You went without me."

Joseph shrugged his shoulders almost involuntarily. Simon was so clumsy. At that moment the professor went by and opened a door. They all followed him.

"You know I've found some very curious books

here," Simon whispered in Joseph's ear. "There's *Martial* with the translation opposite. I'll show you. Some of the passages . . .!"

But Joseph was not listening. In the lecture room the students were choosing their places, and for different reasons sat either near the professor or as far away as possible. David Laud sat by himself in the back row. Joseph's first impulse was to join him, but he thought this might look pushing and sat down unwillingly in the front row. Someone at once asked him to move up and make room; it was Simon Demuth, who reached up to whisper in Joseph's ear.

"I changed classes at the last minute. I'm taking Greek instead of German, so we shall be together."

Seeing that the professor was looking for a list, he added: "We ought to be a bit further back. It's more convenient for the days when we have a test. I'll explain afterwards."

But nothing Simon said affected Joseph, who drew himself up to his full height as though to get as far away from his neighbour as possible. There was too much revolving in his mind and he waited for the professor, as for a magician, to tear him away from himself and from his thoughts. Why had David not suggested that they should sit together? He looked so cold and so pre-occupied now, although a moment ago he had been so cordial. Joseph glanced over his shoulder. He saw a pleasant, serious face, very different from Praileau's. The flame of pride did not burn in David's eyes as in the other's. In spite of himself Joseph recalled the painful scene of the night before, the voice which seemed to lash him like a whip: "You're afraid . . . I'm going to lay you out at my feet." An uncontrollable anger rose in his breast. The veins in his neck swelled and his blood was thumping. Ever since he woke he had been trying not to think of all that, and more especially of Praileau's most wounding phrase: "You're a murderer . . ." A murderer! He had risen early to say his prayers and to read his Bible, seeking consolation in the Psalms and Gospels, but now he was suddenly shaken by this wave of violence.

Someone spoke his name; it was the roll-call. He pulled himself together and said "Present!" but the walls round him seemed to move and his hands were cold. The whole room swam before his eyes from right to left like a ship's deck in a rough sea. He made an effort to attend to the little man in spectacles who was writing the first few letters of the Greek alphabet on the blackboard. The chalk squeaked once or twice and the sound, tiny as it was, was ear-splitting. Joseph got up, pushing Simon, who started.

"May I go out?" he said aloud.

No sooner had he said these words than they seemed extraordinary. In a dark mist he saw a white face turned towards him and a voice answered: "Of course."

He was standing by the open door when the same voice asked if he wanted someone to go with him, but he shook his head.

"No, thank you, sir."

Alone in the library he heard the door close behind him. The large table with the open lexicon . . . He had to go round it to reach the other door. Under his breath he murmured, "I can't . . ." A feeling of giddiness made him rest one hand on the shelves as he moved towards the door. On reaching it he saw he was in the great hall decorated with plaster casts, and remembered a short staircase leading to the basement; he had only to turn right and follow the wall.

The steps seemed to give way under his feet. Supporting himself against the wall, his forehead and cheeks white and damp with sweat, he at last reached the place which mentally he never called anything but 'the place', as the plainer, more exact, word embarrassed him, and stood there swaying and groaning. In the half-light of the basement he could see a skylight and a row of doors cut off at chest level. There it was. He took a few steps and, bent double, his forehead icy, opened his mouth and vomited. His protesting entrails heaved. He staggered, nearly fell and clung to the door. Again the disgusting flood rose to his lips and his stomach, racked with the effort, contracted and then relaxed.

Wiping his mouth with his handkerchief he went over to a wash-basin which he had not noticed at first. The cold water on his face helped to restore him, but he was still panting and whispered, "Oh, God! God!"

A mirror on the wall showed him a face he hardly recognised. His eyes seemed larger on account of the rings round them, and they still held an expression of horror. It was rage that had made him sick. He ran his hands through his hair, arranging it to cover the wound made the night before, and tried to smile. He had better go back upstairs and wait in the hall until the class was over. Whatever happened he would not say what had been the matter; they would think he had been drunk. The thought distressed him; it did not occur to him that one is not drunk at eight in the morning. Most of all he was afraid of what David would think. "I'm looking for the Holy Bible." He remembered his words of a short time before and hid his face, burning with shame, in his hands, but in the last twenty-four hours everything seemed to make him ashamed, and if it were possible to vomit from shame it was from a deadly shame that he had vomited.

He went upstairs again to the hall. On either side of the entrance were two large plaster statues which he avoided looking at as the figures were naked. Instead he looked out of the open windows at the long lawn where ash and sycamore stretched their delicate shadows in the morning light. On either side the small white columns of the covered arcades shone like silver, and at the far end the library with its proud façade and heavy marble pillars formed the background to this peaceful picture.

Joseph wondered if he ought to go back to the Greek class. Perhaps they would ask him if he were ill, and as he did not like to lie it would be difficult for him to answer. He decided to stay where he was until the class was over and then to go on to the English class, which was in the same building. With a movement he could not control his head turned in the direction of the arcade on the right and he looked for the place where last night he had waited for Bruce Praileau to come back. It must have been under that tree whose main branch curved like an arch. That was where he had suffered.

He felt that in the last two days everything had changed. Up to now he had never understood what was meant by a heavy heart; now he knew: a weight in his breast impeded his breathing. He gave a deep sigh. Thoughts like these could only do him harm. The simplest, most Christian act would be to forget his resentment completely and to harbour no further grudge against Praileau. "I'm not angry with you any more, Bruce," he murmured gently.

A burst of laughter came suddenly from behind one of the doors, presumably from students enjoying one of the professor's jokes. The young man's face reddened. He remembered the way Praileau, too, had answered him by laughing, as though to throw his forgiveness back in his face. The whole scene passed yet again through Joseph's mind. It was becoming a kind of obsession.

He turned suddenly round and walked quickly past the statues back into the little classical library, where he turned over the pages of the open dictionary on the table. Was there really anyone in existence who knew what all these words meant? Through the door he could hear the professor's colourless voice and he tiptoed over to listen. A phrase about rough and smooth breathing struck him as odd and he strained his ears to catch the words. Now he was talking about long and short vowels being modified in quantity according to their position in the word. What did that mean? The words penultimate and antepenultimate increased his confusion. If he could not understand the very first lesson how would he manage to follow the course? For some days he had felt the lurking, unacknowledged fear that he was not clever enough to finish his studies. In his little home town he was considered better educated than most other boys because he knew the Scriptures and could easily find any passage quoted to him. Moreover, he expressed himself almost as well as the minister, but it was a very different world at the University, and Joseph felt that all the other students were much better equipped than he was. As he listened to their conversation he could see that they thought quickly and were ready with their answers, whereas he always needed time to think and was constantly short of a reply. He frequently had the impression that they thought him a bit simple and were laughing at him.

He went and leaned against the window, looking at the hills, whose vague outline seemed to dissolve in a glowing mist. The words of the Psalm rose irresistibly to his lips and he whispered them to give himself courage. "I will lift up mine eyes unto the hills . . . He that keepeth thee will not slumber . . . He will not suffer thy foot to be moved . . . He shall preserve thee for evermore." He picked a spray of honeysuckle and again smiled as he breathed in its scent. In moments of trial a blind confidence would suddenly come to him for no particular reason. Sometimes it was enough to think of God for the most obstinate problem to be mysteriously resolved.

A quarter of an hour later a bell made him start and he went back to the hall. All the doors opened at once and the students came out with a great clamour of voices. Some were going to another class; others with nothing to do for an hour disported themselves on the lawn. They could be seen stretching and yawning in the sun in what Joseph considered an insolent way, but he did not have much time to watch them for a hand seized his arm and he swung round.

"There you are!" Simon said in his nasal voice. "I've been looking for you. What was the matter?"

Joseph avoided his questions as well as he could.

"I didn't feel well. Anyway I'm all right now."

Simon squeezed his arm.

"We have an English class right here," he said, pointing at a door across the hall, "but we've two minutes before the bell goes. Have you seen the statues?"

His eyes shone and he opened his large mouth as though to take breath in preparation for further exclamations.

"I don't like them," Joseph said firmly.

"What? But you haven't looked at them properly." Simon cried. "On the right is the Apollo of Phidias. On the left the Hermes of Praxiteles. Hermes is splendid. Look at his curls, his neck, the line of his neck. His neck is like yours, a little . . . And his shoulders . . ."

Joseph walked away without a word. Simon ran after him.

"What have I said now?" he begged. "Don't you see, they are the gods of Ancient Greece. Hermes carries the infant Dionysos in his arms."

"I hate idols," Joseph said, going to the English class.

"But they're not idols for us!" explained Simon in a sort of wail.

He noticed people looking at him and lowered his voice.

"They're simply very beautiful people," he added.

Joseph gave him a withering look.

"Beautiful?" he breathed. "They're naked!"

The nine o'clock bell interrupted Simon's answer and he had to content himself with a helpless gesture.

VIII

THAT afternoon there were no classes and, as they were
free, many of the students left their rooms to go and enjoy
themselves in the town. Joseph installed himself with
his books in what he decided was the quietest corner of
the library. This large, neo-classical building was an
imitation of the Pantheon at Rome, but its inner circum-
ference was reduced by recesses, each with its large
window and furnished with a table and two arm-chairs.
Three galleries gave access to the books, which could be
smelt rather than seen, for they were hidden in the half-
light, though a sickly odour of old bindings and old
paper hovered under the great dark blue dome studded
with gold stars.

From his chair Joseph could see the long brick road
leading to the main gates of the University and nearer
at hand a tall magnolia with its leaves silhouetted black
against the brilliant blue sky. He glanced briefly at the
landscape and opened the copy of *Romeo and Juliet* which
he had just borrowed. He had to read this play and two
others by the end of the week. Joseph sighed. It was
a love story and love stories bored him, but he flattened
the pages firmly with his large hand and began to
read.

After the first few lines of the Prologue his attention
began to wander. What did he care about this quarrel
between two Italian families? And this passion of a man
for a woman, or rather, for a girl of fourteen? His
interests lay in the salvation of souls and where were
these people's souls, if they had ever existed? Assuredly
they were burning. While he was reading their story

in the silent library the two lovers were howling like beasts in the endless pangs of the retributive fire for having thought only of satisfying their desires. Still, he had to read these lines, and many others too. By so doing he would educate himself, since this was how he had to learn.

By a freak of memory he suddenly thought of Simon and of his ridiculous remarks about the plaster idols. Perhaps he had snubbed him too harshly and he was sorry, but he had to stand up for himself and safeguard his time and his work. He had asked Simon to leave him in peace until the next day, and the little man had gone to his room to sulk. Still, he was not there to think of Simon, but to read *Romeo and Juliet*. Clutching his head more firmly, he re-read half a page which he had not quite understood and then plunged with determination into the poet's world.

Half an hour went by in which he did not move except to turn over a page. A ray of sunlight came through the magnolia branches and lay near him on the table like a long sword. Students came and went noiselessly under the dome with books under their arms. Some slept in the afternoon heat, slumped over their tables; nearly all had taken off their jackets and rolled up their sleeves. The day waned slowly.

At about four o'clock someone passed the recess where Joseph was reading, seemed about to stop, hesitated, went on, and then returned, and standing a little behind the motionless student watched him attentively. It was Praileau. For several minutes he stood there without moving, ready to disappear at Joseph's slightest gesture. Something passionate and brooding in his expression made his young face look like that of an older man, and in an indefinable way he might have been said suddenly to resemble his ancestors, for with his ruddy cheeks and large, gleaming eyes under coal-black brows he brought to mind a portrait from some earlier age. His short nose with widened nostrils, his proud, red lips, gave him an aggressive, compelling air. He wore a well-cut dark-brown suit and his tie was knotted with deliberate carelessness. His every attitude betrayed the natural elegance of his slight but strong body. Looking round in case he was observed, he craned forward over Joseph's shoulder to read the title of the book absorbing his attention. A faint smile mounted from Praileau's mouth to his eyes, but he immediately became serious and watched the reader with a look compounded of extreme curiosity and a kind of restrained fury. Seeing him there, holding his breath, his neck stretched out like an animal on the watch, one might have thought he was waiting for a suitable moment to strike his enemy down, but on Joseph's moving to turn a page the hidden watcher started, straightened himself and disappeared.

IX

THAT evening Joseph went up to his room immediately after dinner. This was contrary to all University custom, for even the most studious remained idle until nine o'clock. But he was seized with a fever of learning and he felt, too, that while studying he was protecting himself from what, without being more precise, he called evil.

He stopped before the small mirror and, lifting the

heavy bronzed lock which fell over his temple, looked at the scar on his forehead: it was changing colour, becoming purple, and could not be seen as long as he kept his hair carefully disordered. At the same time he examined his eyes, worried by the rings round them, and his mouth, which appeared to him almost as thick as a negro's. 'Sensual,' he thought sadly. His face was not the one he would have liked to have. There were moments when this white, eager face looking at him out of the black frame horrified him. He wished he had pale, transparent grey eyes, thin lips and a gentle, spiritual expression— a face like that of the minister in his home town. By praying hard, reading the Bible and working he could perhaps, if not alter his features—that was impossible— at least impart to them the marks of an interior life. "A man must overcome his passions," he said, sitting down at his table. But what passions? To tell the truth he had none. When people spoke of passion they meant love and he had never been in love. Although he did not like to admit it, for after all Shakespeare was Shakespeare, the story of *Romeo and Juliet* seemed simply idiotic with its secret love, its violence and double suicide; all grave, perhaps even unforgivable, sins. His own parents had not made all that fuss about getting married! And a decent young man never thought about the unchaste act by which he had been conceived.

He opened a history of literature and with his elbows on the table rested his head on his hands. The last rays of the setting sun touched his dishevelled hair with coppery red and pale gold. Outside, the high wall of brown and purple leaves framed by the window still reflected the light. A slight breeze seemed to be trying

48

to disperse the mass of warm air which oppressed the town. From time to time a porch door opened and shut with a click and students could be heard calling to each other in the twilight.

For a quarter of an hour Joseph had been reading a chapter on the Elizabethan theatre when a murmured conversation in the next room disturbed him and he raised his head impatiently. He thought that by stopping his ears he would find silence, but then a continuous noise seemed to fill the air. Finally he got up, crossed the room heavily and then coughed, hoping to silence the chatterers. But from the other side of the door a monologue, interrupted by muffled exclamations, seemed to indicate a confidential talk. Joseph did not recognise the speaker, but could not help smiling on hearing Mac-Allister trying to get a word in.

"I want to say something. My personal experience . . ."

"Shut your big mouth, Mac," said someone, "and let him finish."

It was Simon speaking and Joseph frowned at his harsh Northern accent. There were sounds of dispute and protest, then the first voice went on in somewhat professorial tones.

"In conclusion, gentlemen, the house I was speaking of will be open to all, in conformity with the wishes of our illustrious founder, and one hundred years after his death."

"Why did they wait so long?" MacAllister asked.

"They simply didn't dare. In the name of decency generations of students have either been condemned to perpetual repression or have indulged in solitary acts. . . . Well, that is just what the great man wished to spare

49

the youth of the future: the nightmare of chastity and all the disorders which result therefrom."

"I shall wallow in it," MacAllister cried. "I shall never be able to wait till next Monday."

"What do you mean by disorders?" asked a voice.

There was an embarrassed silence.

"Let it not be once named among us," said an ironic voice.

Joseph recoiled and sat down on the bed, his heart thumping. The one thing that touched him out of all he had just heard, and only half understood, was this verse from the Bible, which blazed in his head. There were some words which one never uttered, as though in fear of drawing down God's anger. These boys must be mad to bring the Scripture into their filthy talk. Did they even know what they were saying?

Getting up, he put his hands over his ears so as not to hear any more and went to the window. Opposite, lights were burning on the ground floor, which was just visible through the sycamores. Some boys came out on the porch, pretending to fight, and chased each other along the red-brick path. Joseph lowered his hands. A piano near-by was playing "Swanee", the popular song of the moment, at once lively and sad.

"Hey, Bill," cried a voice from the end of the road, "are you coming to the Jefferson with me?"

From inside a room came the question: "What are they showing?"

"*The Sheik*, with Valentino and Agnes Ayres."

"I'm coming!"

For several minutes Joseph listened, without moving, to the voices and the music. Then he turned on his table-lamp. The open book shone compellingly, but the young man no longer wanted to read. All this noise disturbed him. He sat down again on the bed, which almost touched the door of the next room. They were still talking, not so loudly as before, but from time to time MacAllister uttered a sentence in ringing tones.

"I like them small," he declared, "and blonde, rather plump, but not too plump, white as milk and as smooth as . . . as smooth as a plum."

"Smooth as a plum isn't bad," said the scholarly voice. "Where did you get that, Mac?"

"In my own head, of course!"

"*Mollior cuniculi capillo* . . . Catullus didn't do better: softer than rabbit's fur."

The conversation sank again to a confused murmur and whispers. Suddenly these words emerged:

"Boy, you feel as though you were on a wave. See what I mean? It carries you on. . . ."

It was MacAllister communicating his personal experience. Joseph blushed violently; he felt as if all his blood were flowing to his head, throbbing in his temples, and his throat swelled. He raised his hands to undo his tie and the first button of his shirt. It was no good now resting his head on both hands with his elbows on his knees; he had heard. The words were fixed in his mind, never to be effaced, and provoked a succession of pitilessly clear images, and although he closed his eyes, shaking his head as though to chase them away, he suddenly felt himself possessed by the devil.

Almost at once a hand touched his shoulder and, raising his head, he saw a young man smiling at him.

"David!" he cried.

"I happened to be passing," David Laud said, "when I saw your light and came up. Your door was open," he added in apology, "and I knocked, but you didn't hear me."

His voice was soft and rather slow, softer and slower even than it had been that morning, and Joseph had a curious impression of words flowing like oil. He stood up quickly.

"I was thinking," he said, somewhat embarrassed.

David pointed to the book lying open on the table.

"You were studying too, I see. I would advise you to wear an eye-shade when you're working. This light is much too strong."

He looked round and nodded, the corners of his mouth curling in a smile which never left him. At that moment MacAllister's metallic voice rang out again.

"I pay them two dollars, but they've got to earn it!"

Joseph shuddered and turned away so that David should not see him blush, but his visitor was walking round the room and apparently had not heard. There was in all his movements an indefinable mixture of reserve and authority, and one could not imagine his making a blunder. In his beautifully creased navy-blue suit he was rather awe-inspiring, in spite of his pleasant manners. He looked several years older than he was and the expression "young man" hardly suited him, for nothing about him suggested youth, except his unlined face of classical regularity.

Joseph unobtrusively buttoned his shirt and tightened his tie.

"Bring your books to my place," David said, moving to the door. "If you like we can work together."

Joseph turned out the light and followed his companion downstairs. Soon they entered a small street, which was badly lit and still further darkened by an avenue of trees meeting overhead in an arch through which the first stars could be seen. The two young men walked in silence. Above their heads, hidden in the leaves, the tree-toads uttered their clear note and all these little cries mingled in one quiet but piercing song, rising and falling according to some mysterious law, but never stopping. David opened a gate sheathed with wistaria.

"Here we are," he said, leading Joseph along a brick path.

Joseph saw a light, half hidden behind a pillar, and his foot soon touched the bottom step of the porch. There was a noise of chairs being moved and one or two people who could not be seen answered David as he wished them good-night.

In the hall a lamp threw a feeble light on a spiral staircase. David took Joseph's sleeve and guided him the length of the darkened ground floor and opened a door.

"Don't move," he said.

He struck a match and almost at once the room became visible in the golden light of an oil lamp, which threw a great yellow circle on the ceiling. Joseph gave an involuntary cry of admiration, for everything in this room spoke of order and comfort, unostentatious comfort, and just looking round gave him a curious feeling of security. One of the walls was entirely covered with books, whose formal bindings gleamed like bronze, but elsewhere the wall-paper was covered with little pink and blue flowers and gave the room what might best be described as a virginal appearance. There was something about it reminiscent of a young girl's bedroom, in spite of the mahogany table covered with large books, papers and black leather note-books. The narrow bed over in the corner, with its carefully turned-down sheets and pillows placed neatly on top of each other, looked rather prim. On a polished wooden bedside table stood a Bible, with gilded edges, and a large glass of milk—symbols of a quiet mind.

"Sit down," David said.

They sat at the table and without further preliminaries David opened a Greek grammar at the alphabet and gave it to Joseph.

"Read that," he ordered.

Joseph obeyed. David repeated each letter in his warm, steady voice and when they had finished shut the book with his well-kept white hand.

"Now repeat what you've just read."

"Alpha," Joseph began.

He stopped, reddening. He remembered alpha and omega because of Christ's words, but not one of the other letters.

"We'll try again," David said gently.

They began again, but were no more successful the second time.

"I shall never learn it," Joseph said, clasping his big hands and cracking their joints in a kind of fury.

"On the contrary, you're not leaving this room until you have learnt it."

"Why is your room cooler than mine?" Joseph asked, almost aggressively.

"Because mine faces north and yours south. Besides, I

keep my window shut during the heat of the day and only open it at night. Alpha . . ."

"Alpha," Joseph repeated miserably.

At the end of an hour he could recite the alphabet without a single mistake.

"You see," said David.

He went on to the rules of accentuation. Joseph sat still, but he was ill at ease. Although it was, in fact, cooler, the lamp was hot and brought beads of sweat to the roots of his hair. His trousers were tight at the thighs and he would have liked to get up, walk about, raise his voice and stretch his arms. He did not dare; that even, sensible voice kept him in his seat and he listened in spite of himself, watching the round, nickel-plated lamp, which reflected his face. It was odd to see himself so tiny in a room with a distorted, arched ceiling. Joseph could see David reflected too in this convex mirror and their hands were almost as large as their heads. Joseph's hands were more terrible to see than his companion's and he moved them, looking at the lamp to see the effect. Now he could see nothing but his hands; they advanced, and moved about, like monsters and far behind them was his white face, framed in red.

"Are you listening?" David asked patiently.

Joseph stared.

"The antepenultimate . . ." he said.

David's lips parted in a slight smile.

"That means the last syllable but two in a word."

"Yes," Joseph said, his eyes fastened on David's with sudden eagerness. "I'm listening to everything you say."

'This man will save me,' he thought with a glow of gratitude.

It took him several minutes to understand a sentence from the book which David showed him and explained. He was again afraid that he would not be able to follow, but David appeared to read his thoughts.

"You won't have any difficulty in class tomorrow," the young teacher said. "I've gone beyond the lesson, because I wanted to see if you were really interested."

"Oh yes, I am."

David shut the book.

"May I ask you a question? Don't answer, if you'd rather not. It has nothing to do with what we've just been learning."

'He's going to ask me why I left the class this morning and I shan't be able to answer him.'

"No," said David, as though replying to this thought. "I simply wanted to know why you are studying Greek."

Joseph's heart beat a little faster. He found it difficult to answer the question, for he might betray part of his cherished secret. On the other hand, if he said nothing it would mean he was afraid or, what was worse, ashamed.

"It's to read the Gospels," he said at last.

"I knew it," David muttered, adding, "I, too, want to read the Gospels and Epistles. In that way one can get nearer to Christ's thought."

"You think we will be nearer Him?" Joseph asked suddenly.

"Certainly, from an intellectual point of view."

Joseph got up.

"Intellectual?" he repeated. "I want to see and touch Him."

"What do you mean?" said David. "Faith should be

enough for us all. Besides, who has seen Christ since His ascension into Heaven?"

"I want to be near Him, do you understand? As one is near a living person. And I want to see Him."

There was a silence. Joseph tucked his grammar under his arm.

"I must go back," he said. "Thank you for helping me."

David rose, too, and touched the young man's arm with his finger-tips.

"Have you ever thought of taking orders?" he asked.

Joseph shook his head vigorously.

"No," he said. "Never."

"I shall begin my theological studies as soon as I have my degree," David said, joining his hands in a gesture that was already clerical.

There was another silence.

"You are lucky to have your life all mapped out for you," Joseph said shortly.

"I heard Christ's call."

Their eyes met; neither wavered.

"How did you know it was He?" Joseph asked. "Was He standing by you?"

"God speaks to the heart in an unmistakable way."

Joseph's only answer was to raise his eyebrows. He was becoming embarrassed by the turn the conversation had taken and was seeing David in a different light. He was rather sorry he had come.

"It has just struck eleven," he said. "I must go."

"Come and see me again," David said, smiling.

He went with him in the dark to the garden gate and, pressing his arm, murmured, "Remember what I said about God's call."

"Sure!" Joseph said.

He strode back along the streets. The night was full of delicious scents and rather unwillingly, as though it were not really right to do so, he breathed the heavy perfume of the honeysuckle which mingled with the fine, bitter smell of dead leaves. In spite of the warm air October was heralded by these heady scents which provoked a vague, almost physical, happiness. But Joseph was uneasy and discontented. In his conversation with David he had made several remarks without being able to stop himself and without even knowing where they came from. For example, that idea that he wanted to see and touch his Saviour, as Thomas did after the Crucifixion. . . . He had never thought of it in his life, but once he had uttered those extraordinary words he was forced to repeat them, so that it would not seem that he was weakly changing his mind. He had wanted to say something striking, something remarkable, and that was what had come out. David had taught him his lesson for an hour and a half as though he were a child. That was the reason. He wanted to show this self-confident man with his Greek alphabet and his antepenultimates that he, Joseph Day . . . But what had he wanted to show him? He stopped suddenly. He no longer liked David so much, particularly since the last few minutes of their conversation. Joseph admitted the obvious good intentions of this serious-minded student; he was even grateful in an exasperated way, but David humiliated him by not talking as man to man. Even his smile betrayed a secret condescension and when he spoke of God he joined his hands. All this was insupportable.

Back in his room he threw himself on the bed, without turning on the light. He lay there for some time face down, his head in his arms. Obviously the people at the University thought him ridiculous. Every time he spoke to one of the students he said something odd which aroused surprise or contempt—yes, it was contempt for his ignorance and country ways. He had guessed this and it hurt him. What was he trying to do, anyway? To save souls! Fortunately he had never yet said to anyone: "I want to save you!" But one of these days he would say it and be covered with shame. Nothing could prevent him, for words like these came straight from his heart, in spite of himself.

With a sigh of annoyance he got up and crossed the room to turn on the light. What he saw drew an exclamation of surprise from him. On a pale blue sheet of paper on his table a large magnolia flower revealed its depths of pearl and snow. It was still living, but would soon fade; the tips of some petals were already stained with brown. With a sudden, uncontrollable gesture Joseph snatched it to his face, greedily pressing the soft, white mass to his eyes and mouth. The perfume intoxicated him; he breathed it, drank it in, holding the flower in his cupped hands, as though to lose nothing of its freshness and scent.

He remained motionless for more than a minute. An inexpressible sadness mingled with his pleasure, for the flower he crushed and killed gave him an immense longing for happiness which he could not explain.

59

Suddenly he threw it away, muttering: "What's the matter with me?"

His eyes fell on some words scribbled across the pale blue paper: "Less white than thou . . ."

At first he did not understand and with a frown re-read the phrase, which at last became clear. It was about himself and the flower. A practical joker was comparing him to the flower which now lay at his feet. Who had dared? . . . it must be that idiot Simon. He was sure of it; he recognised the half-wit's style. His cheeks flushed with shame and he tore up the paper and was about to throw the flower out of the window, but as he held it in his hand, which trembled with rage, he was struck with the literal truth of the phrase which had upset him. The crumpled petals were indeed of not so pure a white as his own flesh, and his skin, in particular the fine skin of his fingers and wrists, at once dull and shining, emulated their lustre. 'What does that prove?' he thought. 'What's the fool getting at?' And raising the mosquito screen at the window he threw the flower into the street.

Then he read a chapter from the Bible and knelt down to say his prayers. Turning out the light, he undressed and went to bed, but it was a long time before he could sleep.

X

THE next few days were passed uneventfully in study. Joseph was gradually becoming accustomed to every aspect of his new life. Each evening he worked in the library, which remained open until eleven, in order to escape his neighbours' obscene conversation. He was still afraid of being unable to keep up with his studies and so learnt the most difficult lessons, in particular the Greek, by heart. He was then able to be independent of David's kindness, although the latter offered every day to help him.

One morning as they were leaving the biblical literature class the future minister made a sign to Joseph that he wanted to speak to him. They were both free until the end of the morning and, putting his arm in his friend's, David took him quietly aside on to the cemetery road, where Joseph had walked that evening with Praileau. When they had passed the last houses David cleared his throat (just like a parson, Joseph thought) and began to speak.

"Please believe that what I am going to say to you is in your own interest. I have a great affection for you," (here he pressed Joseph's arm) "and I want to be of service to you. In life's struggle we cannot despise the advice of our equals. . . ."

He went on in this strain for some minutes, words piling on words, without Joseph discovering what he was trying to say. They walked slowly under the trees, along the hedges covered with honeysuckle, and the song of a solitary lark filled the deep blue sky.

"The appearance one presents to the world is not without importance," David went on sententiously. "We are judged by our manners, our speech, and by our attire. Will you permit me to make a few personal remarks?"

This question was purely rhetorical, for without giving Joseph time either to consent or refuse he went on.

"Your manners are irreproachable. You speak

61

correctly and you never blaspheme, as do so many others. Moreover, thank God, you do not drink. Added to this your face is . . ." He hesitated for the first time, trying to find the appropriate word, and coughed discreetly behind his hand. "Your face is pleasing. You can thank heaven for all this, but there is one thing I have noticed."

A momentary pause underlined his next remark.

"Your dress is a little careless. It is probably not your fault, but the suit you are wearing has seen better days. The cuffs are frayed . . ."

Joseph reddened as if he had been struck.

"I should say it's not my fault!" he cried. "I'm poor. My parents . . ."

"Don't get angry," David said, suddenly voluble. "I don't want to annoy you. I want to help you, do you understand? If you want to buy a new suit I can advance you the money and you can pay me back later. We could go to the tailor now. I know one in town."

"No," Joseph said. "I don't want to."

David took both his hands and, looking into Joseph's flashing eyes, begged his pardon. Joseph was taken aback. An affectionate impulse could always disarm him; in him tenderness and anger lived side by side, and he had a sudden desire to embrace David, but checked himself. His face was lit by a smile.

"I know this suit is very old," he said, "but I have only one other, which I keep for special occasions, such as a visit. Besides, I left it at home, so as not to be tempted to wear it here."

David nodded and gently resumed his discourse. Joseph must learn to stand up for himself, otherwise the world would take advantage of his simplicity, laudable though it was in itself. At this point the simplicity of the dove was invoked, but joined with the wisdom of the serpent. It was completely justifiable to wish to meet one's adversary on equal terms. Now, by appearing in sartorial disorder one was discredited in the eyes of that redoubtable adversary, the world. Sad to say, even the most worthy people entertained these unjust prejudices.

"Do you think they do?" Joseph said.

David was sure of it. By degrees he made his companion turn round and they heard the University bells ringing far off in the peaceful air. A more beautiful, more golden day could not be imagined, and Joseph felt a sudden affection for life and for all human creatures, an obscure love for everything around him—the trees, the red soil, and David, whose serious profile stood out so clearly in the sun that riddled the leaves with its rays.

"David!" he cried, "aren't you sometimes happy without knowing why? It makes me want to laugh, as children do, for no particular reason. . . ."

"Children do, yes, but in our world there are too many problems for us to laugh like that. You and I have not the right to be heedless."

They walked on in silence for several minutes. When they came in sight of the gymnasium, shining large and pink in the sun, Joseph asked: "Why did you say 'You and I' just now?"

David gazed out above the trees.

"Because God has chosen us," he said.

Joseph said nothing, but his heart beat faster and he repressed the words which rose to his lips. They went on to the building where the Greek class was being held. They still had five minutes. Passing the plaster Hermes and Apollo with averted eyes, they entered the small library.

"I forgot to mention," David said in a low voice, "that there's a vacant room in my house. It's more or less like that one I have. If you'd like to take it you'd be quiet there. There's only an old lady in the house, a Mrs. Ferguson, and two maids, who go home in the evening. No students."

"No students . . ." Joseph repeated.

"Yes. From some points of view that's an advantage. I've asked them to keep the room for you, so let me know as soon as you can."

He showed his fine, regular teeth in a coaxing smile, as he added: "We'll go to the tailor soon, won't we?"

A bell rang, the classroom door opened and the students came out, chattering.

Under cover of the noise Joseph said: "I could never pay you back for the suit, David. Better give up the idea."

"Yes, you can," David said, pressing his arm. "I'll explain later. You'll see."

XI

THAT afternoon Joseph and David boarded the little red street-car which was taking the film-going students into town; but the two young men were not going to the cinema. While the youthful passengers, packed on the platform, shouted and laughed, David explained to his companion the plan he had in mind. From time to time, when someone jostled him in getting off, or when he heard a particularly offensive oath, he closed his eyes with a long-suffering air. With a careful hand he re-adjusted his little black hat on his head and continued his discourse.

"This restaurant will open in October for the students and one or two outside people. It's quite a new idea. You help yourself. You get a tray and cutlery when you come in and then choose your dishes at a buffet. It's what's called a *cafeteria*. Students will be paid for clearing the tables and for . . . looking after the crockery."

"You mean for washing up?" Joseph asked gloomily, for he was beginning to understand.

"That's it!" David cried, his eyes sparkling as at a piece of good news.

They said nothing more until they had reached the town. In the street David took Joseph's arm, but the latter immediately freed himself.

"I've noticed that it makes some people laugh," he explained.

"*Honi soit qui mal y pense,*" said David.

Although he did not understand, Joseph did not ask for an explanation of this sentence.

"How much should I be paid for washing up?" he asked abruptly.

"I don't know yet, but if you don't like the idea of working in the cafeteria I will wash up with you."

This was said with so much gentleness that Joseph blushed, ashamed. David always had a disarming phrase at the right moment.

"I didn't say I didn't like the idea," he murmured.

A few minutes later they entered the tailor's and were shown some materials. Joseph wanted black, but David preferred navy blue, which, in his view, was suitable for every occasion.

"No," said Joseph, determined this time not to give way. "I want black."

He was shown into a little fitting-room, but then the trouble began. Without giving any explanation he refused to be measured for his trousers. David and the tailor looked at each other and raised their eyebrows. Finally Joseph consented to try on a ready-made suit, as long as it was black. A dark grey one was found and rejected.

"You could always have it dyed," the tailor suggested, smiling, "since you insist on black."

David thought this a very good idea. Joseph, who could not think how to object to this absurd scheme, was forced to assent to it and retired into the fitting-room. He soon came out, looking fierce, in the suit, which to his way of thinking was too fashionable.

He came forward, his arms half out, glaring at the sleeves, which were a little long. David had a sudden impulse to tell him how handsome he looked, but he bit back the words in time and merely remarked: "The suit might have been made for you."

"We can shorten the sleeves," said the tailor, walking round Joseph with a piece of chalk.

He suddenly went down on one knee and asked: "The trousers are not too tight?"

"Not at all," Joseph said, recoiling.

With a sigh of relief he went back to the fitting-room, tore off the new suit and resumed his old one, grateful for the feel of its well-known creases. A triple mirror showed Joseph the image of a young man, at first furiously waving his arms and raising each leg to get rid of the hateful garments, then suddenly calm at the familiar sight of himself in his everyday suit of cheap, shiny material. He stopped suddenly: he was seeing himself in profile for the first time and although he always felt suspicious of mirrors he could not help looking at this new face, but at once became depressed. The profile, indeed, was too like the full face; the nose turned up slightly, the mouth was too full and too red; these were not the features Joseph would have liked. And yet it was he, himself. He sighed; then, making sure his hair covered the scar, he rejoined his companion. 'He, at least, does not look sensual,' he thought.

As he entered his room he saw Simon, who was turning over the pages of a note-book on the table with a kind of artless effrontery.

"What are you doing in my room and why are you reading my notes?" Joseph demanded in a voice that trembled slightly.

"Oh, Joseph!" cried the little man, throwing the note-book aside, "you frightened me. You always frighten me when you talk like that. If you only knew . . ."

"Answer me!"

"There's nothing to answer. I was waiting for you. I was looking at your note-book."

"Why?"

"I was wrong. I'm sorry. I was wrong."

He clasped his hands in a theatrical gesture. Joseph

jumped, as though hit below the belt, and threw his hat on the bed.

"Simon," he said, "was it you who put that flower on my table last night with that ridiculous note?"

"Ridiculous?"

"Yes, ridiculous. I forbid it, do you hear?"

He was panting with anger.

"Naturally I tore your note into a thousand pieces and threw the flower into the road, in the dust. I hate that kind of joke."

His eyes glistening with tears, Simon planted himself before Joseph, working his lips as though about to speak. Then he went to the door and disappeared without having uttered a word.

"What's the matter with him?" Joseph wondered, tidying his papers. "What's the matter with all of them? Why don't they leave me alone?"

The new suit was the chief cause of his bad temper. As usual David had got his own way. David was always right.

He sat down at the table and buried his face in his large hands. Gradually his irritation subsided. He wished so much to be kind, to speak gently, but something unexpected always prevented him and upset him. People hardly ever behaved in the way he expected and everything they did and said shocked him; he could not understand them. Even David, with his perpetual smile. And as for Simon . . .

'I was too hard on him,' he said to himself. 'I'll speak to him later. But he's so stupid with his flowers and his notes.'

For several minutes he abandoned himself to a daydream in which his most shadowy thoughts seemed linked in a way he could not understand. He kept on seeing himself under the trees at night, confronting Praileau, who hurled contemptuous words in his face. He tried vainly to dismiss this humiliating picture from his mind. In one way or another everything seemed to bring him back to it.

David and he had walked home to economise and he felt tired. He could easily have gone to sleep with his head on his arms, but he would not give way, and he decided to go over his English literature lesson while the house was still quiet. He opened his Shakespeare. Next day's written test would consist of three questions to be answered within five minutes, simple enough questions, but precise, and dealing both with the art of the play-wright and with the language of the period. He turned the pages of *Romeo and Juliet* uneasily and ran his eye over several passages which came between the love scenes, for although he would not have admitted it it was the love that he disliked. His eye was suddenly caught by four lines which he could not understand. He read and re-read them carefully. The words were not archaic, but the sentence was obscure. To the young man's surprise the notes threw no light on the speech. Elsewhere they were copious, almost unnecessarily so, but here, where enlightenment was needed, they were silent. Supposing he had a question on that passage tomorrow? Perhaps David would know? But he did not want to ask David.

Why had David said that they were both chosen? What did he know about it, this cocksure little man, who talked as though he were in the pulpit? He even held his head stiffly, as though wearing a starched clerical collar;

and then there was that restrained, patient voice and that affable smile, ready for each comer . . . Was that religion? 'I prefer an untamed religion,' he thought suddenly. He closed the book sharply. What upset him most was that David had forced his hand in this business of the new suit. He had got round him with his fine words and pious arguments, and had proved that in the interests of religion Joseph ought to dress like a gentleman, although Amos and Hosea and the Apostles and Christ Himself must have been poorly dressed. An untamed religion, that was it. Folding his arms, he gazed gloomily at the opposite wall. His mind was made up: he would not go back to the tailor to try on the suit, he would not even argue with David, since David by using unexpected arguments always got the upper hand in a discussion. Quite simply, without losing his temper, he would say: "No!"

He spoke the word aloud, firmly. It rang out in the silent room and aroused him from his reflections. With an impatient gesture he opened his book and, with his elbows on the table and his hands thrust in his hair, plunged almost grimly back into the story. The lovers' cooing seemed both indecent and monotonous; he thought it improbable that any human being would rave like that. In the hands of poets love became a piece of solemn nonsense; no responsible person could really believe in it.

He was so absorbed by these thoughts that he did not hear Simon come in. The latter stood for a moment, undecided, in the middle of the room with his sketch-book under his arm, looking at Joseph with a mingled expression of delight and fear. Finally he coughed gently and whispered: "Are you still angry with me about that magnolia flower?"

"Oh, it's you," said Joseph. "Of course I'm not angry. But let me get on with my reading."

Simon came a step nearer.

"Will you let me stay if I don't move and don't open my mouth? I'll sit over there in your arm-chair and draw your portrait."

"Draw my portrait!" Joseph cried. "Never!"

"Oh, why not?" Simon wailed, his eyebrows raised.

Joseph slammed his fist on to the table.

"Because I don't want you to!"

Simon came closer, joining his hands, like a child.

"You don't understand. I must draw, so as to learn my profession, and I need a model. The other fellows send me away. It bores them. But I don't even ask them to stay still, they could go on reading or writing. But they don't want to. Listen . . ."

"What do you do with your . . . portraits? Do you show them to people?"

Simon looked keenly at Joseph.

"Never," he replied.

They looked at each other in silence.

"You wouldn't like me to try and find a woman model," Simon resumed, meekly.

"No, indeed!" Joseph said, and he added suspiciously, his eyes alert: "I get the impression that you're often thinking about women."

At these words Simon, his eyes gleaming, laid his left hand on his heart.

"On my honour, Joseph, I never think about them at all. I swear it!"

71

"All right," Joseph replied, reassured. "You didn't have to swear. You should never swear. Sit there and get on with your work, but let me read."

'He's a good boy,' he thought, as Simon drew a pencil-case from his pocket. In the silence could be heard the light scratching of pencil on paper, large strokes first for the outlines and for the eyes and mouth, then shading —a great deal of shading—for the hair and shadows. The artist half-closed his eyes, took measurements with his thumb, rubbed out, blew on the paper and fidgeted in his chair, secretly hoping to attract attention, but Joseph gradually forgot his presence. After ten minutes Simon coughed almost inaudibly and whispered, as though he wanted to be both heard and ignored: "I spent yesterday evening with a remarkable fellow, who is very anxious to know you. We were talking about you."

Joseph turned a page without answering. A sigh of impatience escaped Simon. He contemplated his model for a moment and muttered something inaudible.

Then he began to whisper again, rubbing the paper with his finger to soften a shadow.

"It's the Latin tutor who wants to meet you. He's very clever. He noticed you the other day in the classical library." He added anxiously in a lower voice: "I asked him to come here this afternoon."

"What are you talking about?" Joseph cried suddenly, slapping his hand down on the table. "How do you expect me to work if you keep on chattering?"

The terrified artist leapt for the door.

"I'm sorry!" he wailed.

Joseph motioned him to return to his seat.

72

"Don't keep on telling me you're sorry. Say what you want to say and have done with it."

"Well," said Simon, perching on the edge of the arm-chair, "the Latin tutor, a remarkable fellow, quite remarkable, says he wants to know you. You see, you interest him. He saw you the other day, he watched you—oh, he's very observant . . . He and I spent the evening talking about you."

"Why?"

At this icy question Simon's eyes widened and rolled from side to side in fear, apparently looking for an answer in the air around him.

"Why?" he repeated, guiltily. "Because . . . well, anyway, why not?"

Joseph folded his arms and looked inflexible.

"Because I don't know this tutor of yours. How can he spend an evening talking about someone he doesn't know?"

"But you will know each other," Simon said timidly, raising his sketch-book as though to shield his face. "He'll be here in ten minutes. I told him to come at five."

Joseph got up so abruptly that he nearly knocked the table over.

"Now listen, Simon," he said, with menacing gentleness, "you'll make me lose my temper and you'll be sorry."

Simon ran behind the chair, letting his album fall on the floor.

"No!" he cried in an altered voice. "Don't look at me like that. I shall cry all night again!"

"Cry, you idiot?"

At this moment MacAllister came in, as impertinent as

73

ever, his hands in his pockets and a little green hat perched like a halo on top of his head.

"You *are* making a row!" he said, in his loudest tones. "You can be heard in the street. You should have seen Agnes Ayres in *The Sheik*," he went on in the same breath. "There was one scene where she was practically naked in Valentino's arms. The pianist forgot to go on playing."

Joseph shrugged his shoulders and sat down, but Simon was disconcerted and did not move.

"What's the matter with you?" MacAllister asked.

Catching sight of the album, he seized it before Simon could stop him.

"Give me back my album!" he cried.

But MacAllister was already at the other end of the room, safely behind the head of the bed, and was carelessly turning over the pages, his head on one side and his eyebrows raised.

Simon, very pale, approached the foot of the bed.

"Listen," he said in a stifled voice. "If you don't give me back my book . . ."

"What will you do?" asked MacAllister, examining a drawing with half-closed eyes. "Stop speaking to me?"

He turned over several pages.

"I'll kill you," Simon whispered, clutching the brass bed rail.

"Then the sheriff will hang you and you will go and burn in hell."

"That'll do!" said Joseph, getting up.

MacAllister gave a shout and brandished the album, his eyes shining with malicious glee.

"This is marvellous!" he said. "A portrait of Joseph

74

with eyelashes like a film star . . . This'll kill me! Joseph, have you seen how handsome you are? Here, catch!"

The album flew across the room and landed at Joseph's feet. He picked it up.

"Get out of my room!" he ordered.

With his hands in his pockets MacAllister went to the door, swinging his hips, and in a falsetto voice began singing "Rose of Washington Square", which was all the rage at the University. Simon stopped his ears.

"Shut the door," said Joseph, when they were alone.

The little man obeyed, then collapsed on a chair.

"I wish I were dead," he murmured, hiding his head on his arms. "I'd have liked to tear out MacAllister's eyes, but I didn't dare. I'm a coward."

There was a long silence.

"Take your book," Joseph said, sitting down.

With a kind of yelp of grief Simon got to his feet.

"You're furious with me!"

"I didn't say so. I told you to take your book."

"Did you look?"

"At the sketch you did of me? Yes, I did."

"Haven't you any comment?"

"No, I've told you once, I'm no judge."

He slowly turned his black eyes on his companion, whose olive skin had taken on a curious grey tinge, and for a moment they looked at each other. Simon held his breath.

"You despise me," he said at last.

"Are you crazy? Why should I despise you? I don't understand what this is all about."

Simon came forward and, leaning against the table, gazed into Joseph's large, dark eyes, trying to fathom his

75

thoughts. His heart thumped horribly; he could feel the violent pulsing in his throat. With an effort he let go of the table and stood up.

"Listen, Joseph," he began. "You must try to understand. I don't feel well. I'm suffering. I'm suffering at this moment."

"Sit down if you're not well," Joseph said. "Perhaps it's the heat. I'll get you a glass of water from the bathroom."

"No, stay here."

He made a gesture and sank into the arm-chair, which began to rock him maternally. A few seconds went by. Joseph cracked the joints of his long, thin fingers, then folded his arms. Then Simon again hid his face and began to cry.

"I've no courage," he moaned. "I ought to speak to you, but I can't. I'm afraid of you."

Joseph did not reply at once, but moved the books about on his table and then said: "If you don't mind, I'm going on with my work. I must finish reading *Romeo and Juliet.*"

Simon raised his face glistening with tears.

"How can you understand *Romeo and Juliet?*" he asked in a voice broken with emotion.

Joseph looked offended.

"I understand it perfectly," he said. "There are explanatory notes at the end. I've been held up by one passage, but I'm going to read it again more carefully."

Without covering his face this time, Simon wept, and the chair creaked as it rocked. The little man could hardly have realised how ugly he was in his grief. His drawn forehead and his nose furrowed by little parallel wrinkles made him look as if he were about to sneeze, and large tears caught in his eyelashes and then rolled down his cheeks to the corners of his open mouth. From time to time he sniffed gently.

Several minutes went by. Joseph turned the pages of his book, pretending to read, with one elbow on the table and his hand in his hair. Suddenly he got up and went over to Simon, saying nothing but looking at him with an air of faint distaste.

"Simon, men don't cry," he said at last.

Simon gestured with his small, brown hand, as though brushing away an intruder, and replied hoarsely: "You don't understand, Joseph. You don't understand anything."

As he said this he got up suddenly and the chair began to rock vigorously.

"Why do you talk like that?" Joseph asked.

Simon was already at the other end of the room. As he faced the door he seemed to gather his strength and managed to say in a stronger voice: "You'll suffer, too, some day. You'll see then what it's like!"

XII

JOSEPH was completely overcome by this scene. Alone again, he walked up and down his room, muttering: "The fool! What did he want to come here for? I'm sick of his affairs! I'm sick of the lot of them!" In an undertone he added: "I'm sure Simon was lying to me. He may swear as much as he likes, but he's no better than the others. He's just like the others." He coloured, as though about to say something improper. "Yes, they're all the same. They all think about women! Simon as well!"

This last remark relieved and reassured him. It was as though it were the answer to a difficult question. He expelled the air from his lungs in a deep sigh, but his face clouded over. 'Perhaps I should accept David's offer to move in,' he thought. 'At least I should be left in peace.'

"But then there'll be David," he said aloud. "David with his arguments and his advice."

His eyes fell on the rocking-chair, which was still in gentle motion, and he remembered Simon's words, but waved his hand, as though to chase them away. He did not like thinking about this queer boy and yet he could not help seeing him in that chair, weeping—just like a girl! What could you say to a man who was weeping? And then that ridiculous sketch of himself, which made him look like a cinema poster!

He stood in the middle of the room with his hands behind his back, looking at the little street with its red-brick pavements strewn with yellow leaves. The first floor of the house opposite could now be seen through the almost bare branches. There were young men there too, perhaps, full of anxious questions about themselves and about others.

'I wonder if he is saved,' he thought suddenly. From all eternity God knew where Simon would go after death and there was no changing it. Even supposing that Simon's thoughts were not occupied by women, which was not certain, he did not behave according to Joseph's ideas on the conduct of the small band of the

78

elect. Simon lacked any air of spirituality; in fact he was excitable, capricious, unreliable. One might almost have said that he did not *look saved*. His words and actions were not only surprising, they were sometimes shocking. Joseph thought of the album skimming through the air to land at his feet, and the recollection disturbed him. He could almost hear Simon's voice of restrained anguish: "You don't understand. You don't understand anything." What was it that was so difficult to understand? Suddenly he realised that the sweat was running down his forehead.

Half an hour before dinner someone knocked gently at his half-open door and came in without waiting for an answer. The newcomer was a tall, angular man, whose dark-green suit hung loosely on his spare body. Plus-fours showed his thin calves in stockings of a brighter green, and horn-rimmed spectacles gave him a scholarly look. His wide, smiling mouth revealed a row of extremely white, long, even teeth, which contrasted with his swarthy complexion. He came over to Joseph with hand outstretched.

"Edmund Killigrew," he said in a nasal voice, which Joseph immediately recognised from having heard him a few days before quoting Latin in the next room. "I expect Simon told you I would be coming, but I'm a bit late. I was held up by a Faculty meeting."

He held the young man's hand in his for a few moments before shaking it.

"Call me Edmund," he said, sinking into the rocking-chair, "or Ed, if you like. I'm sure we're going to be chums."

Joseph sat at the table, more upright than usual, and folded his arms.

"You were talking in the next room a few nights ago," he said coldly.

"I expect I was," Killigrew said with another smile.

He whipped a gold case from his pocket, like a conjuror, and held it out open to Joseph.

"Cigarette?"

The young man shook his head with a hostile air and watched his visitor take a cigarette in his yellow fingers and close the case almost insolently, turning the costly object over in his hands, as though to draw attention to it, before he put it back in his pocket. The next instant a long green holder was in the corner of his mouth and, blowing a cloud of blue smoke towards the ceiling, Killigrew rested his right foot on his left thigh, with his hand on his ankle. He began to rock himself slowly.

"You don't smoke?"

"Never!"

"Haven't you tried?"

"I don't want to try."

"Repressed," Killigrew muttered to himself. He shook the cigarette ash on to the floor and said: "You know I'm the Latin tutor. If I can ever be of service to you . . ."

Faced by Joseph's silence he became more serious.

"You know, Joe, there are several of us who take an interest in you. The other evening we had a long talk about you."

Joseph remained perfectly still.

"That may seem odd to you," Killigrew went on.

"It's true we hardly know each other and you don't make friends easily. Still, people talk about you. One can see with half an eye that you're not like the others."

"I don't feel any different from the others," Joseph said with a shrug.

"Ah!" cried Killigrew with a triumphant twang, "that's precisely the crux of the matter. You refuse to recognise the difference. Now you know as well as I do that the students think of nothing but women and drink, whereas you . . ."

"I certainly don't!" Joseph cried, unfolding his arms.

"You do too," Killigrew said gently. "You, as well as the others."

Joseph got up so abruptly that he knocked over the chair he had been sitting on.

"That's not true!"

"Now, now," said his visitor calmly. "Don't act like a child. Pick up your chair and let's have a chat. The difference between you and the others is that they give way to their instincts. . . ."

"Their bestial instincts," Joseph said, red with anger.

"Bestial, if you like. There's a beast in every one of us."

Joseph was about to exclaim: "Not in me!", but something stopped him. He was afraid of looking a fool in front of this man who was better educated than he was and who smiled knowingly at almost every sentence, as though he had just said something particularly subtle. He stooped and put the chair back on its legs, but did not sit down.

"This conversation . . ." he began suddenly.

He stopped. Killigrew rocked himself and watched.

"This conversation displeases you," he said quietly at last.

"Yes."

"Very well, Joe, let's talk about something else."

Joseph sat down.

"I've taken a liking to you," said Killigrew with a rather crafty expression. "I wouldn't offend you for the world. If I have, I'm sorry and apologise."

"Oh, you haven't offended me!" Joseph said, on an impulse he could not repress. "I like you too."

This was not quite what he had wanted to say and he bit his lips, but he was always disturbed when he heard someone acknowledge his faults and he tried, clumsily, to repay Killigrew for his admission. If it had not seemed an absurd gesture he would have shaken his hand.

"What were you reading when I came in?" Killigrew asked with an air of great interest.

"Shakespeare's *Romeo and Juliet*. What a pity you're not the English tutor too! There's a passage here I don't quite understand."

A self-satisfied laugh greeted this naïve remark.

"Read it just the same, my dear Joe, and we'll see."

Joseph found the passage and, bridling a little, read several lines in a voice which was an unconscious imitation of an old-fashioned preacher. Killigrew's lip curled in a diabolical smile.

"You read beautifully," he said when Joseph put the book down.

He put on a professorial air and his voice became harder and more nasal.

"The passage in question may appear obscure," he said. "Many editors in the last century omitted it because of its licentious character, but it is quite clear what Mercutio has in mind. He is talking of Romeo's erotic dreams as he sits under a medlar tree thinking of his naked mistress and, as the text has it, of her 'etcetera'. Etcetera is delightfully hypocritical, a false concession to modesty, for it is far more suggestive than the frankly crude word which it covers with a transparent veil."

Joseph got up.

"Is that really the meaning of what I've just read?" he whispered hoarsely.

"Precisely, Joe."

Seizing the open book in both hands, the young man tore it in two and threw it furiously on the floor. Killigrew rose.

"Joe—" he began.

Joseph turned to him, his face inflamed; his eyes shone like steel and his lower lip shook.

"What do you want?" he cried in a voice of thunder.

Without answering Killigrew went out.

XIII

JOSEPH ate no dinner that evening and by eight-thirty was ringing at the mathematics professor's door. He had to wait for some minutes in a small, mahogany-furnished parlour which looked out on to the lawn bordered by sycamores. By standing sideways in a corner of the room he could see, between two Doric columns, the dark green door at which he had knocked on that night, now so distant, although its memory still distressed him, and he regretted his unwise impulse of curiosity. It would be better if he never thought of Praileau at all, better if he could erase from his memory that name which only provoked him to resentment. On the other hand, he felt it was his duty to pray for his enemy and even now he pressed his hands tightly together, thinking: 'O Lord, grant Praileau Thy blessing!' But he was ashamed by his lack of fervour. In vain he gripped his fingers almost to breaking point and closed his eyes till he frowned; deep down in his heart there was no desire to see a heavenly blessing fall on Praileau. What he most wanted was to break his jaw.

"What a hypocrite you are," he murmured, letting his arms fall. "You pretend to forgive him, but there's no real forgiveness in you."

He gradually became calmer and sat down in an armchair near the lamp; then he got up again and stood with folded arms before the glass-fronted case filled with books in gilt-embossed bindings. Addison's *Spectator*, in ten volumes, stood next to Dryden's complete works. In a prominent position a large Shakespeare, bound in tan-leather, made the young man wince and he left the bookcase and began to pace the room. Suddenly the door opened.

"I didn't expect to see you so late," Mr. Tuck said as he came in. "You're welcome just the same, but what serious business brings you here?"

They sat down.

"Nothing serious," Joseph said, blushing.

"In that case you could quite well have waited till tomorrow and seen me in my office."

Pursing his lips as he spoke, his stomach lifted by his short breath, the professor leant back in his arm-chair.

"I'm listening, Mr. Day."

Joseph lowered his head as though this would help him to find the words he wanted, but he was afraid to open his mouth. He suddenly saw how stupid it was to disturb a professor at that time of night to tell him that he wanted to change his classes. Mr. Tuck was perfectly right; he should have waited until the next day. But now he was there he must say something to justify himself.

"Today," he said suddenly, raising a face still red with embarrassment, "I behaved . . ."

He tried to think of an adverb, but failed. A patient smile encouraged him to continue.

"I tore to pieces my copy of *Romeo and Juliet* . . ."

After a second he added: ". . . by Shakespeare."

The professor merely raised his eyebrows.

"Yes," Joseph went on more firmly, "I don't like this play and I refuse to study it. When I say I tore it to pieces," he explained, anxious to speak the literal truth, "I mean I tore it in two."

There was a silence.

"From which I infer," the professor said calmly, "that you want to take another course instead of modern English."

"Yes, another English course."

"You have the choice between Anglo-Saxon and Middle English."

"I know," Joseph said. "I'll do Middle English."

"Chaucer, isn't it?"

"Yes, Chaucer."

With an effort Mr. Tuck heaved himself out of his chair and stood up. Joseph at once rose.

"I believe you told me that you were studying Greek so as to read the New Testament in the original."

Joseph nodded.

"I'm sure you have solid reasons for not wanting to go on with the modern English course. It's years since I read *Romeo and Juliet*. Poetry is not my business and, between you and me, Shakespeare bores me. But to tear up a book . . . here of all places, Mr. Day! At the University!"

The student folded his arms.

"Nevertheless it's what I did."

"There's nothing to be proud of," Mr. Tuck replied more sharply.

Joseph looked at him without answering.

"I hope you're a man of moderate habits," the professor went on.

"I live as one should."

"Not too much alcohol, eh?"

A flame shone in Joseph's eyes.

"No drop of alcohol has ever passed my lips," he said huskily. "I don't even know what it tastes like."

Mr. Tuck looked at him, then put a hand gently on his shoulder.

"You know," he said, smiling, "for some years now I've been the mentor of a good many students. You can tell me everything, for it's part of my job to receive confidences. If you are in any difficulty . . ."

"I have no difficulties, sir."

"What made you tear up that book?"

Joseph threw back his head.

"Well, I came across a passage so indescribably indecent that I lost my temper . . ."

86

"I don't remember any such indecencies," Mr. Tuck murmured, letting his hand fall.

"Some editors omit them," Joseph said with a knowing and somewhat cunning expression.

"Quite possibly. But you're severe, Mr. Day. I don't know if you realise it, but Chaucer didn't exactly write for a girls' school. What do you intend doing later on?"

"I don't know yet."

"What are you most interested in?"

The young man's features hardened and he hesitated; at last, with a serious expression, he replied: "Religion."

The professor lowered his head, pulling at one ear, and appeared to be thinking.

"No offence meant, but you're still very young," he said in a friendly tone. "Your ideas are interesting and I see you're no trifler where morals are concerned. But in spite of that, if you ever do anything very stupid, as young men do, you know, remember I'm here to help and advise you."

"I sincerely hope never to do anything stupid."

"I hope so too. But at your age the most important thing in life is love, and love makes one behave very stupidly."

Joseph replied patiently: "Mr. Tuck, the most important thing in my life is religion."

"Well, Mr. Day," said the professor, slapping him jovially on the back, "so much the better. Tomorrow I'll enrol you for the course you've chosen."

As he spoke he guided Joseph gently into the hall and they parted.

XIV

BEFORE going back to his room Joseph went to see David and found him in his room sitting at his table, which was covered with papers and dictionaries. A broad, rather mechanical smile lit his calm face as he looked up from his books.

"No, you're not disturbing me," he said, in reply to a question from Joseph. "You never disturb me. Sit down there, opposite me."

Joseph brought a chair up to the table and sat down.

"I shan't stay long," he said. "I've really nothing to tell you, but I wanted to talk to someone."

David joined his hands on a dictionary, as though it were a Bible, Joseph thought.

"If you had the room I told you about, the one at the end of the corridor, we should be able to enjoy each other's company."

Joseph nodded. In the lamplight his face seemed to become a gold mask, pierced by the large black holes of his eyes. There was something so striking and noble about his features that David suddenly exclaimed: "You do look . . ."

But he suppressed the adjective that came to his lips, just as he had in the tailor's shop.

"What?" Joseph asked.

". . . pale," said David, lowering his eyes. "And you seem anxious."

In a few words Joseph told him of his difficulties with Shakespeare and his visit to the mathematics professor.

"Was I wrong?" he asked when he had finished.

"Wrong to change your class? No, you've a right to."

There was a pause, then Joseph asked, rather hoarsely: "Was I wrong to tear up that filthy book?"

David pondered.

"One should have read Shakespeare, but I'll give you an expurgated edition some day. I can't really approve of your tearing up the book. And yet . . . listen, Joseph, the world is unclean and one must be resigned to it."

"No," said Joseph, rising. "To be resigned to the world's uncleanness is to deny the Gospel."

"There's no question of that," David said, also rising. "You live in the world because God put you there."

Joseph's eyes flashed.

"I hate the world, do you hear? Christ said that he did not pray for the world. The world is damned."

Turning on his heel, he went to the door. Without speaking, David accompanied him to the end of the garden, where the moon spilled pools of wan light between the black shadows of the sycamores. David put both hands lightly on Joseph's shoulders.

"In essentials we both think alike," he said quietly, "but one must win souls by gentleness and patience and, in a sense, seduce them."

"Seduce them!" Joseph cried indignantly.

"You must try and understand me," David went on, lowering his voice. "You are so uncompromising in your honesty that everything is suspect in your eyes. One must fight the Devil with all the weapons God puts in our hands."

"With a scourge, like Jesus in the Temple."

David did not reply and Joseph stood there, at once proud and embarrassed by what he had just said, and not knowing how to take his leave.

"You know," David murmured, "we have the same faith, the same hope, and I love you like a brother, a brother in Jesus Christ."

Joseph made a movement.

"I know," he said in the slightly husky tone which with him indicated a sudden emotion.

He wondered if he should press David's arm, but instead he moved back a step. His heart was thumping. He forced himself to smile at the young man, who watched him gravely, leaning against the iron gate, where the flowers stood out in black and white in the moonlight.

"Yes," he said awkwardly, "you're right; we believe in the same things. Thank you for saying that."

"Good-night, Joseph," said David.

As Joseph was crossing the road he added in a louder voice: "Think over your answer."

Joseph turned round.

"What answer?"

"About the room. And another thing. We're going to the tailor tomorrow afternoon. I'll call for you."

These last words came out all in one breath as David shut the gate. Joseph saw him wave his hand as he went back up the path, but this friendly gesture received no reply.

XV

TEN o'clock was striking as Joseph entered his room and he decided that he had time to prepare his history lesson before going to bed. It was no use. With his head in his hands he gazed at the open book, but his attention kept on wandering. For one thing, he was annoyed with David on account of his remark about the tailor, which wiped out the good effect of everything he had said before. It was just like that shrewd, practical little man! Too shrewd. He wanted to seduce souls! But Joseph was principally angry with himself for not having spoken about Simon, which had been his sole reason for going to see David. Once more he had said something quite different from what he intended, when it was so easy to confide in someone who liked him. But why did David always irritate him? 'An untamed religion,' he thought. 'What he wants is a domesticated religion with white bands and well-kept nails.'

He suddenly shut his book and went down the passage to knock at Simon's door. There was no answer, but MacAllister's trumpet tones came from the next room.

"Simon's in town. Who wants him?"

He came out in his shirt-sleeves and leant against the door jamb, with his hands in his pockets.

"Ah," he said carelessly, "it's the exterminating angel."

"Why do you call me that?"

"It's not me, everybody does, you big fool. It's no good looking at me like that. I'm not a bit afraid of you. Here, come in and have a drink. I get bored drinking by myself."

"No," said Joseph and moved away towards his room.

"What do you want Simon for?" MacAllister asked, without stirring.

Joseph stopped.

"I want to talk to him."

"You'd better go gently," MacAllister said, slowly coming up to him.

"I don't understand."

"Precisely. You don't understand anything."

Passing Joseph, he went into his room and threw himself face down on the bed with his head on the pillow.

"Get out of my room!" Joseph ordered.

MacAllister looked at him sideways with half-shut eyes.

"Would you like me to tell you something about Simon?" he asked confidentially.

Joseph hesitated, then moved to the head of the bed, his hands on his hips.

"Well, what is it?" he said.

"Simon is a sick man."

"Sick? What's the matter with him?"

"The matter is that he's queer. Odd, if you prefer it. For all the horrible details see Killigrew: he'll give you his long lecture on Freud."

"Freud?"

"And if you're very good you'll also get the speech on Plato, Michael Angelo and Shakespeare."

"I don't understand."

"I don't understand," MacAllister repeated, mimicking Joseph's serious tones.

He shut his eyes as though in sleep, but his mocking profile still seemed to defy the tall, silent young man.

"Go away!" said Joseph.

"Why don't you take advantage of my presence to try and save my soul? You can preach me a little sermon. I'll be quite quiet, I shan't snore too loud. And thanks to you I may have wings and a harp one of these fine days."

"How can you laugh at such things?" Joseph exclaimed, his neck red with anger.

"You know, Joe," MacAllister continued, with affected innocence, "we're going to have a good time in town tomorrow night. You ought to come too. There'll be a reception in the fine red house on the corner of Jefferson Street, near the station. The ladies will serve drinks to the students. After that they'll dance with them. Do you want to know how, Joe?"

"I don't know what you mean."

"Of course not, but I'll show you."

He at once began to jig up and down on the bed in such a suggestive way that Joseph's ears burned. Without a word he unbuckled the black leather belt round his waist and, holding it like a whip, raised his arm. And he felt, as he had when striking the tree in the woods with a branch, that his arm was acting of its own accord. The narrow strap whistled down through the warm air on to MacAllister's back. He threw himself off the bed with a howl. A second blow cut into his legs and he gave another cry of rage and pain.

"You wanted a sermon, here you are!" Joseph said in a stifled voice which he himself did not recognise. "Do you want me to go on, son of Belial?"

His victim glared at him with hate and muttered: "No!" The silence was broken only by the breathing of the two young men, who looked at each other open-mouthed. At last MacAllister got up and managed to reach the door, with his back against the wall and his knees sagging. His white face expressed mingled terror and surprise and his jaw hung trembling, as though he had forgotten to close his mouth. During all this time their eyes never left each other and Joseph imperceptibly turned his head, following the movements of the son of Belial until he finally disappeared into the corridor.

Mrs. Dare's sharp voice was lifted in the silence.

"If you please, Mr. Day!"

Joseph came out of his room and went to the head of the stairs, still holding his belt as though it were attached to his hand. Footsteps mounted a few stairs, then Mrs. Dare's head appeared behind the banisters, somewhat ruffled, her cheeks covered with rouge and her eyes bright.

"I merely wanted to remind you that your room is above mine."

She caught sight of the belt and raised her eyebrows. 'Another fight!' she thought. In a gentler voice she added: "That's all, Mr. Day. Good-night!"

He murmured something and bowed. Mrs. Dare's head vanished.

Back in his room, Joseph shut the door and, throwing down the belt, covered his smarting eyes and hot cheeks with his hands. Those cries had been overheard. Mrs. Dare had heard them. It was practically a scandal.

"I did it for MacAllister's own good," he whispered through his fingers.

But a voice inside him breathed: 'It wasn't him you wanted to thrash.' Without moving he said: "David."

Ah yes, David! That fellow annoyed him too with his sermons, his protective manner, his . . . 'No,' said the voice. 'Someone else.'

Joseph still did not move. 'I have sinned,' he said to himself. 'I should have driven MacAllister out of my

94

room, not thrashed him. I had no right to do it. I shall beg his pardon, whatever it may cost me.'

'Someone else,' said the tiny, implacable voice. 'It was another man on whom you wanted to be revenged. You know his name.'

"It's not true!" Joseph said aloud, letting his hands fall. "I've forgiven him; I never think of him."

'His name is Praileau,' said the voice, and was silent. The young man shuddered. Everything around him seemed so peaceful; the books under the lamp, the rocking-chair in its corner, the window open on to the night—cooler now, but filled with the song of the tree-toads. Joseph felt strangely uneasy. He looked over his shoulder, as though expecting to see someone, but there was no one there.

Without even turning off the light he threw himself heavily on the bed and at once fell asleep.

XVI

He gloomily put the big parcel containing his new suit on a chair.

"You can put it on tomorrow for church," David said with a smile.

Joseph was tempted to thank him ironically for his permission, but he controlled himself and said nothing, for after all David was paying for it! But the little parson had got his own way again and had made Joseph do what he wanted.

"I like your room," he said, looking round approvingly. "If it weren't for your . . . regrettable neighbours."

Joseph knew what he was hinting at and did not reply. He wanted to be by himself. But since the suit had placed him under an obligation to the man, he could not get rid of him and resigned himself to putting up with his unwelcome visitor, though this did not prevent him from casting angry looks at the pale blue box with its red string.

What annoyed him even more than this affair of the suit was that he had weakly confided all his personal troubles to David, or rather, David had drawn him out as they were going to town (on foot, for the sake of economy). And David, who never talked about himself, now knew the whole story about Simon, not forgetting the ridiculous detail of the magnolia, together with the incident of MacAllister and the disgraceful thrashing. If only he could take back his words, erase all recollection of his indiscreet chatter from the mind of this imperturbable little man! For he had put himself in David's hands and although David had gently rebuked his violence towards MacAllister, he had not delivered judgment in the case of Simon, merely tightening his lips. If only he had exclaimed: "Bravo, Joseph! You did the right thing!" But no, only a cautious reserve, an old man's reserve. Thank heaven, Joseph had not mentioned his dispute with Praileau!

"Well, I'll leave you to your work," David said after a moment, taking up his hat. "We'll meet again tomorrow morning at eight. Remember they're giving Holy Communion."

"I know," said Joseph.

David moved towards the door.

"Thank you for having confided in me," he said.

"Thank you for lending me the twenty dollars," said Joseph sharply.

The moment he had said this he was sorry and turned to the door to call David back, but he was already going downstairs, and two other students were coming up, talking loudly. After a moment's uncertainty Joseph shut the door and went back to his table.

He read the whole of the fourth chapter of St. Matthew, then the fifth chapter as far as verse twenty-four. At this point he stopped reading and looked out of the window. A fine rain glistened on the large yellow and red leaves strewn on the pavement of the little street, and the first scents of autumn floated into the room. In the house opposite a young man was studying near his window, like Joseph, but he did not raise his head from his work.

"First be reconciled to thy brother," murmured the young man.

The Book spoke as though he, Joseph, were being personally addressed. Its voice was like no other voice ever heard, always saying words that went straight to the heart of a problem, but sometimes what it demanded was very difficult and in this instance impossible.

"Impossible," he said as he rose. But he was ashamed at the sound of the word. One could not say no to the Book. The Book was there on his table, repeating the same words which it would repeat for ever, and nothing in the world could prevent its being so; it could not be silenced. "First be reconciled," it said, not to just anyone, but to Joseph in particular, as though Christ had entered his room and had sat down to speak to him.

He felt that he was about to yield, because he always

97

yielded to the Book, as he did to men, too, if he thought he heard an echo of the Book in their speech. But this time he could not yield. No doubt that was why he had this choking sensation which made his hands go to his throat; he was going to do something impossible—not tomorrow, but at once. It would not be easy to find the right words; he would have to lead up to it, he would invent a pretext, begin by talking about something trivial. . . .

For several minutes he remained glaring in the middle of the room. He did not want to go and apologise to MacAllister, because at the bottom of his heart he despised him.

Suddenly he left his room and went down the passage. The door was open and he went in.

MacAllister was lying on his stomach on the bed, his head in his hands, reading a copy of the Police Gazette, whose pink pages were adorned with photographs of naked girls, but on hearing Joseph he raised his eyes and sat up, wincing with pain. Without saying a word, he left his bed and moved into a corner of the room. His small white face was again filled with terror, which seemed to flow from his eyes and spread over all his features. Joseph tried to smile and wanted to speak, but he could not think what to say, not having expected such a reception. At last he managed to open his mouth and said in an uncertain voice: "I've come to be reconciled to you."

MacAllister did not move. Joseph waited a moment, then went on in firmer tones: "I've come to ask your pardon."

The sound of these words had a peculiar effect on him;

he had the impression that someone else had said them and that his heart was opened by them. He had an impulse of affection for the man he had insulted. He took a step forward.

"I should not have struck you," he said warmly. "I was unjust, I misused my strength. I want you to forgive me, I want to make amends for the harm I did you."

MacAllister, motionless against the wall, did not reply.

"I don't know why I struck you," Joseph went on. "Sometimes I lose my temper and then I don't know what I'm doing. Do you understand?"

Faced with MacAllister's silence he was at a loss. He could not go on asking his forgiveness. It began to look ridiculous and the Book did not say what one should do in these circumstances. After a hesitation he took another step and held out his hand to MacAllister.

"Give me your hand," he said gently.

But MacAllister's two hands were flat against the wall and remained in that position; his small grey eyes were fixed on Joseph's black ones with the same shocked expression of the previous evening. After a moment Joseph smiled sadly and let his hand fall.

"That's that," he murmured. "I'm going."

With an awkward gesture, which he could not explain even to himself, he touched MacAllister on the arm and left the room. As he went down the passage to his own room a voice inside him cried 'That's too simple! You strike your neighbour as hard as you can with a belt and afterwards go and ask his pardon. He was right not to take the hand you offered him. It's too simple!'

He tottered, as though from a heavy blow, then went back to his room. There, less in order to pray

99

than from self-loathing, he fell on his knees by the bed and hid his face in his folded arms.

XVII

Two people were missing at dinner that night—Mac-Allister and Simon. The silver candle-sticks lit their empty places, but Joseph asked no questions. He sat very upright, gazing over the head of little John Stuart at the other end of the table, who seemed to be trying to hide behind his large spectacles, almost dying of shyness whenever he was spoken to. Near him Skinny, the country boy, was silently gulping all the food put before him, and laid down his fork only to brush aside the long strands of black hair which almost hid his forehead. Hardly anyone spoke. Only George, the tall, pale boy with a freckled nose, sometimes uttered a dogmatic opinion on the respective merits of various footballers. He was a thin, uncouth young man, whose small, lively eyes held an unpleasant expression. He sometimes made sly allusions which escaped Joseph, though they made the country boy laugh. Towards the end of the meal he poured himself a large glass of water and said: "Mac-Allister won't be bored this evening. He's down there now."

Joseph pricked up his ears at MacAllister's name. He would have liked to know what George meant by "down there".

"I shan't go," the country boy said with his mouth full. "For one thing it's too expensive and for another I don't want to give away money to the doctors."

George threw back his head, swallowed his glass of water and got up to go. With a vicious smile he stretched himself and said: "One can't always follow the advice of .at old miser, Benjamin Franklin."

"Benjamin Franklin?" repeated the other.

"Yes, dimwit: 'It's cheap; it's safe; it's agreeable.' "

A burst of laughter greeted this quotation, but George, indifferent to his success, merely made a contemptuous face and left the room, squaring his shoulders. There was a silence after he had gone and Joseph, who had not fully understood these remarks, suddenly asked: "Where's Simon?"

"I've no idea," said the country boy, getting up to leave in his turn.

Two other boys went out with him.

Left alone with John Stuart, Joseph repeated his question.

"Simon has left," the little man murmured in a stifled voice, folding his napkin.

"Where has he gone?"

Stuart made a gesture of ignorance and disappeared.

XVIII

He was once more in David's room, where he felt so at ease, where everything spoke of security and comfort, spiritual comfort as well as material. There, in some inexplicable way, he really felt sheltered from the world. The calm, reassuring light shed by the lamp in the middle of the table was reflected from the bindings of the books on the shelves and from the gilt edges of the Bible at the head of the narrow bed.

The two young men were standing face to face. Joseph's head was lowered and David held both his hands.

"I don't want you to apologise," David repeated. "It makes me terribly ashamed. In any case you didn't offend me just now. You couldn't. I know what you're like. Your intention is always good. Look at me."

Joseph raised his eyes.

"I want to ask you a question," he said.

"Well, what is it?"

"Did I behave properly towards Simon? Was I fair to him?"

David signed to Joseph to sit down.

"Simon is unbalanced," he said, joining his hands and looking very embarrassed. "I was told all about him the other day. It would be as well if you discouraged his visits. Unfortunately you live in the same house. If you lived here . . ."

Joseph leaned forward in his chair and looked David in the eyes.

"Did I behave properly towards Simon or not?" he demanded.

"You didn't act wrongly, but you are exposing him to danger."

"What do you mean?"

David bit his lip.

"I can't answer you, Joseph, at least not this evening. I must think about it, ask advice. Pray for Simon," he added, "pray for him often."

Joseph rose abruptly, anger flashing in his eyes.

"I know what you're thinking about," he said. "People think I don't understand. It's stupid. I understand perfectly well. I know."

"Well, don't let's talk about it," David said hastily. "Let's not ever talk about it. There are some things one shouldn't talk about."

"I shall pray for Simon," said Joseph more calmly, "but I know that no fornicator will enter into God's kingdom, because the Scripture says so explicitly. All these fellows with their women are simply children of wrath."

"Their women?"

"Well, of course. Why the surprise? Do you think I'm half-witted? It's all very well for Simon to tell me he doesn't think about women. He thinks about them just like the others. This evening they've all gone into town, to that house MacAllister told me about, a house . . ."

At these words David sat up, and with a visible effort at control said: "You mean the brothel?"

"Yes. And I'm sure Simon's there at this moment."

David did not reply at once, but looked at Joseph with bewilderment.

"One must not judge others," he said finally. "Christ has told us not to judge. At our age this instinct is almost irresistible, the . . . sexual instinct."

"I loathe the sexual instinct," said Joseph in a hollow voice.

He stood near the table, clenching his fists, the upper part of his face lit by the lamp. A wave seemed to break over his features. With restrained violence he went on: "Did you hear what I said? I loathe the sexual instinct. Do we give way to it? This blind force is evil."

"Not always."

"Yes, always. We're conceived in a paroxysm of madness. Do you think I don't know what happens? It's disgusting."

"But Christ was present at the marriage of Cana."

"What has that to do with it? He dined with sinners, too, and accepted the worship of a fallen woman."

David remained silent. After several moments Joseph went on in a lower voice: "The day I came here Mrs. Dare told me I had a lot to learn. She was right: I knew nothing. But I've been learning. You'd be surprised to know all I have learnt in ten days. I was mistaken about mankind. I wanted to save souls. Yes. That strikes you as absurd, I expect."

"Oh, no!" David said, getting up. "I saw all that in your eyes and it was what attracted me to you."

Joseph recoiled slightly.

"All souls are sunk in the mire," he said, stiffening. "Few of them are saved."

"We can't tell."

"On account of the flesh, few are saved."

David came round the table and stood before his visitor, looking at him for some time without speaking. Then with a shy gravity he asked: "Shall we say our prayers together?"

Joseph inclined his head. With an instinctive movement David turned out the lamp and the two young men knelt side by side in the darkness. They recited the Lord's Prayer together, ". . . lead us not into temptation, but deliver us from evil. For Thine is the kingdom, the power and the glory, for ever and ever, Amen."

They remained kneeling in silence. No sound came

from the world outside. After some minutes Joseph suddenly asked in a husky whisper: "When we were out walking the other day you said that you and I were chosen. Do you remember?"

"Yes."

"Why did you say that?"

"Because I am sure of it."

Joseph waited a moment, then said in the same tone: "We are constantly before God, but at this moment I feel that we are before him in a more special way. I want to ask you a question."

David did not reply and after another silence Joseph asked: "If one is not certain in one's heart of being saved, is one saved all the same?"

"Faith gives that certainty," David murmured. "He who believes is saved."

"But can one believe and still not be sure of being saved?"

David hesitated.

"Are you speaking of yourself, Joseph?"

There was a pause, and the answer came almost inaudibly.

"Of myself, yes."

" 'He that believeth in me hath everlasting life,' " David quoted. And he added slowly: " 'Let not your heart be troubled. Ye believe in God, believe also in me.' "

In the dark his hand sought Joseph's and pressed it.

"Let not your heart be troubled," he said in lower tones. "The Scriptures cannot err. You believe. You are saved."

"Would it be tempting Heaven to ask for a sign?"

"You believe and you pray. That is a sign."

Joseph said nothing. His eyes were growing used to the dark and he could distinguish the white sheet on David's bed and at the window the muslin curtain, waving softly in the night breeze. His spirit was calm; he wished David would go on talking and that he himself could speak in the darkness, which gave their words a serious, religious sound. He had indeed misjudged David, or rather a new David was revealed to him, more evangelical, simpler than the rather condescending young man of every day.

His eyes were closed and he clasped his hands fervently and felt his whole being unburdened, melting into an unknown happiness. Nothing in the world mattered now, except this sudden joy filling his heart and dispelling his grief, and instead of his usual cares he experienced a wonderful sense of security.

PART II

I

THAT night Joseph was woken by a drunken student singing under his window and at the same time he heard voices in the next room. Drawing the covers over his ears he tried to go to sleep again, but whatever he did the sound of the conversation reached him, mingled with the maudlin voice in the street. Every Saturday evening it was the same. The week ended in a drinking bout, which went on until the dawn, and from his neighbours' speech Joseph guessed they had already drunk a good deal. But Killigrew, whose nasal tones he recognised, still expressed himself fairly clearly.

"There's no way of knowing," he repeated.

"But I know!" MacAllister cried. "I tell you Benton still is, and Stuart too, of course, and Dennis . . ."

"How can you tell?" Killigrew asked.

"By their way of standing, walking, sitting down, talking, laughing, smiling, eating, opening a door, whistling . . ."

A burst of coarse laughter covered the end of the sentence. In spite of himself Joseph listened. There was a short pause, then a sentence was uttered by a dogmatic, contemptuous voice.

"A male virgin is ridiculous."

"A male virgin is a man who is afraid of women," MacAllister trumpeted. "And a man afraid of women is no good to anyone."

Joseph instinctively raised his hands to his ears, but he

was ashamed of his cowardice and jumped out of bed. He thought of banging on the door to silence them, but was restrained by the thought that in a few hours he would be receiving Communion and he did not want to lose his temper. He stood there in the dark, dressed only in his night-shirt, which came almost to his knees. 'If they could see me . . .'·he thought. And he imagined the laughter his appearance would provoke, but at the same time his heart beat faster, as though at an approaching danger.

"You can be sure that before the year's out all the men in the University will have been there," said a voice blurred with drink.

"I bet you they won't!" cried MacAllister.

"With the exception of some future clergymen," said another voice.

"Idiot! They're precisely the most dissolute."

"What do you mean—idiot!"

Joseph heard a chair overturn, then Killigrew's voice high and cutting: "Now, you're not going to fight! You're talking about things you don't quite understand. Some men shun prostitutes because of the fear of disease, others because . . ."

"In any case," someone interrupted, "there's one man you'll never see there. You know who I mean."

"If you don't speak more quietly you'll wake him up," Killigrew said.

Joseph's face burned suddenly; they were talking about him. He clenched his· fists and moved nearer the door. A short silence followed Killigrew's remark, then a student murmured: "Oh, that one!"

This was apparently accompanied by a gesture, for

they began to laugh and someone said in a mocking voice: "Angels have no desires."

"Angels!" said Killigrew in his most disdainful tones. "He's made of flesh and blood, like all of us, but he's backward, that's all."

"Or repressed," suggested a youth who had not yet spoken.

"No," Killigrew answered. "Repression comes later; for the moment his sexuality is . . . asleep."

Ribald laughter greeted this remark. Recoiling a step, Joseph again nearly covered his ears and was again ashamed to, for by stopping his ears he was running away. Perhaps he could profit in some way by listening to these men, but he was afraid it might be a sin. Some of the words that reached him through the door seemed meaningless, but for all that they had a strange sound. They reproached him for being backward. Was that an allusion to his studies? But what did repression mean? And that mysteriously indecent phrase about his sleeping sexuality?

Suddenly he fell on his knees by the bed and with his hands in his hair tried to collect his thoughts. 'God, make them stop talking,' he thought. But he listened in spite of himself.

"With a face like his he could have all the women he wanted," someone said in a quiet voice.

"Praileau is better built," said MacAllister.

Joseph started.

"Praileau is merely better dressed," Killigrew said.

Why were they talking about Praileau? Did they know there was something between them?

"A lot of women can't bear red-heads," stated MacAllister.

"I'd like to see the woman who couldn't bear this one," said another voice. "Oh boy! he'd take her round the waist . . ."

With a bound Joseph was in the middle of the room and, seizing the chair on which his clothes were folded, he hurled it at the door. In the half light he had time to see his trousers and jacket leap like living things, then a dull crash seemed to fill the whole house.

There was complete silence, then in a tone of affected concern Killigrew asked from the next room: "Did we wake you up, Joe?"

Before he could answer, the young man heard Mrs. Dare calling him from the foot of the stairs. He opened the door, but did not dare go out because of his bare legs.

"Yes, ma'am," he said gently.

"What's going on?"

"Nothing," Joseph said.

With a slight quiver in her voice she said: "I'm sure you're fighting."

"No."

A second or two went by. Murmuring a few words of apology, Joseph went back into his room, closed the door with extreme care and, jumping into bed, pulled the covers round his ears and shut his eyes. Next door the whispering began again, but he did not listen and was soon asleep.

II

THE next morning he got up early and went to take a cold bath. Everyone in the house was still asleep and he was careful to make no noise, not to splash the water, nor to sing, as he would have liked, but silently soaped his large white body, which he carefully avoided looking at.

When he got back to his room the first thing he saw was the box containing his new suit; the other, the everyday suit, was lying on the floor near the chair the young man had thrown at the door. Joseph would not have hesitated for a moment between the two suits if he had not promised David to wear the Sunday one for the first time that morning, but he sighed as he opened the long box and carelessly tossed its contents on the bed. The idea of having it dyed black had been gently scouted by the future clergyman when he had paid the tailor's bill; it would cost too much and the grey was already so dark. . . . Joseph had not insisted, on account of the money, since there was already that consideration between them, but he had had to master his irritation.

He got dressed. The trousers were, in fact, tighter than he had thought; on the other hand, the coat might have been made to measure, a fact which could be verified by a glance in the little mirror over the fireplace. Joseph did not prolong this examination, which seemed to him to reach the bounds of what was permissible, for more than a few seconds. Then, turning aside his head, he stood there not knowing what to do in these clothes which he thought too fine for him; then he walked to the window, his face lit by a smile of which he was quite unconscious. Suddenly a thought struck him: 'Your prayers!' His face reddened as though someone had hit him. He had not once thought of God since he awoke. It was the first time for years that this had happened and it was like a shock in his breast. At the same time he remembered the strange happiness he had known the night before, kneeling by David. In the light of the morning this took on a different aspect.

"It's a sign," he murmured, not daring, however, to pursue his thought and to see in the mysterious joy a pledge of salvation.

A sign, perhaps, a reply to the anxious questionings on the state of his soul.

Now he was standing by his bed. Seven o'clock sounded from a neighbouring church clock, then further off and more leisurely, from the library. He had fifty minutes before him in which to say his prayers and read a chapter of the Bible, but he did not move. A curious thought had just come into his head and worried him. Looking down at himself, he considered his suit, its rather stiff material still uncreased, except for the trousers, where each leg—with what elegance!—was divided by a straight line. His eyes were fixed on this line. With a sudden decision he unbuckled his belt and let the garment whose perfection intimidated him slide down his long legs. Folding it carefully he placed it respectfully on the chair (though just now . . .), locked his door and knelt down by the bed. But he had hardly said more than a few words when his scruples returned. What sort of appearance was he presenting to God? A jacket on and his legs bare. How could he explain such a strange dress? He could, although the answer humiliated him: fear of creasing his trousers had led him to this outlandish action. So it was vanity . . . Filled with shame, he rose.

Kneeling again, this time decently dressed, he remained in prayer longer than usual, from a spirit of mortification.

He stayed there for a quarter of an hour, his face hidden in the sheets, his hands over his ears, as though to protect his head from all earthly sounds; his hair, which in its depths was almost black, made a dark patch on the whiteness of the bed.

When he got up again he had made his decision: he would leave this house and take the room David offered him. He would then no longer be disturbed by the blasphemies of his neighbours, and he would not lose his temper. There were souls to be saved elsewhere and he would save them by patience, by that tenderness which, at the sight of certain faces, swept over him like a tide of sweetness. Why did they resist him? All his difficulties with other people arose because he could not make them understand the extreme peril of their situation. But he was not a good speaker; words were his enemies and came to his lips with difficulty. Indeed, sometimes he said things he did not want to.

"And yet Moses could not speak either," he said, "Jeremiah too. . . ."

He opened his Bible at Psalm 119, letter Beth: 'With my whole heart I have sought thee.' This passage brought to his eyes tears that seemed to gush from the depth of his heart. What a silence was around him! The little town still slept. The mild October sun touched the red-brick pavement, which seemed immediately to catch fire between the many-coloured leaves. Joseph felt that this was being given particularly to him since he was alone in enjoying the peace and the light, and, lowering his eyes again to his book, he had for several seconds the certainty of being saved.

Nearly a quarter of an hour went by, when there was a

tap on the door and Joseph remembered that he had locked it. He got up and opened. It was Jemima, one of the two negresses who worked for Mrs. Dare. Steel-rimmed glasses gave an air of wisdom to her old face, whose sallow skin shone like oil. Raising her gentle, serious eyes she murmured: "Mr. Joseph, let me do your room. I won't disturb you."

He wanted to send her away, but changed his mind before her humble, animal glance and she came in, tiny in her black dress, a broom in her hand.

"It's always that much done," she explained, going to the bed. "I'll do the other rooms when I come back from church . . ."

With her long, thin hands she pulled back the blankets and sheets and shot a glance at the student, who had sat down again at his table. He was not looking at her. No need to turn the mattress in that case, but almost at once she jumped, for without looking up Joseph said: "Do you read your Bible every day, Jemima?"

"Every day!" she said, seizing the mattress and turning it.

A little nettled, she added: "I was reading my Bible before you were born, Mr. Joseph."

He went on reading without answering, and several minutes went by during which the sheets and blankets went back on the bed, then Jemima shook the pillow into shape.

"If all the other gentlemen in the house were like you," she said gently, "life would be easier for everyone."

Joseph wondered what the correct reply was and could think of nothing.

"They all drink and swear, but you don't," she went on.

'It's not just to flatter you, but cook was saying the other day that you looked like an angel."

He blushed and turned over a page, pretending not to have heard. Jemima moved her broom listlessly round the furniture. Then, for the sake of talking, she said: "In Miss Moira's time the bed was almost in the middle of the room, and a bit sideways."

Joseph raised his eyes without moving his head.

"Miss Moira," he repeated.

"Yes," said Jemima, "Mrs. Dare's adopted daughter. You have her room. She has it during the holidays. For example at Christmas, when you won't be here. Only she likes the bed almost in the middle and a bit sideways. The young lady has her fancies. Haven't you ever seen her, Mr. Joseph?"

"I? No."

"That's right. She left the day you came here, you missed her by a few hours. You would have liked to see her. She's pretty, Miss Moira is, but she has her fancies. And another thing . . ."

This sentence remained in suspense, as though she hoped to be questioned. Joseph had lowered his eyes again to his book and, clenching his teeth, pretended to be absorbed in his reading, waiting for Jemima to go. As soon as she had left the room he rose and slowly turned to the bed, looking at it in silence. The cigarette case he had seen on his first day had been hers. She smoked. And she had slept in the bed he slept in now. A strange silence was suddenly around him and in him.

A quarter to eight sounded at the end of the road, interrupting his thoughts, and he opened a drawer and took out two little books of prayers and hymns in one black cover. He would be early for church if he left now, but he could not stay a moment longer in that room.

III

Two hours later, however, he was back there again. The little books of devotion were thrown into the drawer and the new coat tossed impatiently on the bed. Why did everything have to go wrong on a morning like this? At church the minister's sermon on unworthy Communions had horrified him. The text had been St. Paul's words about "he that eateth and drinketh damnation to himself". Could one be sure, could one ever be sure of not eating and drinking damnation to oneself while communicating, when even the angels were not pure in God's sight? By what sign could one tell that one could safely approach the bread and wine? The Israelite who had touched the Ark to steady it had been struck dead. In the same way the sinner exposed himself to spiritual death unless he had been washed in the blood of the Lamb and completely purified of all his sins.

He had been afraid. When it was time for Communion, David, who was near him, had touched him to get his attention and whispered: "We are going to Communion together." "But I am not receiving Communion," Joseph had replied with a sudden resolve. Without another word David had gone to the altar with a little group of ten or twelve young men.

Why had he given David that reply? He could not have said. The words had been spoken before he had time to think and having said them he could not take them back. 'I ought not to.' This sentence, which he repeated to himself, seemed to have a meaning and to be a reply to every objection. His anger of last night had been a sin, and this morning . . . Since this morning he no longer felt the same. The certainty of being saved had once more given way to the unmentionable fear and, as though the Devil had already taken possession of him, on leaving church he had spoken sharply to David, who asked him again about the room, and faced with this over-serious young man's insistence, he had suddenly refused his reasonable offer. David had merely smiled and pressed his arm, saying that he understood. If only he had lost his temper. But David never gave way to anger, never lost the superiority which set him apart.

Joseph walked round his room with his hands thrust in his pockets. His trousers were too tight. He hesitated to sit down, afraid of an accident, and he would have lain down, except that one did not lie down at ten o'clock in the morning. He would remain standing, read standing, and tomorrow he would put on his old suit and every-thing would return to normal.

Motionless, he fixed his eyes on the bed, looking at it disapprovingly, and for several minutes he was absorbed in a meditation which drew his long eyebrows together and hardened the sinuous lines of his full mouth. Finally, in a flat voice, detaching the words with an effort, he said: "I shall not sleep in that bed again."

This decision seemed to calm him. Placing his Bible open on the mantelpiece he read several pages, but was soon distracted by the noises in the house; in the neigh-bouring rooms students were getting up, calling and laughing. With a sigh he shut the book and was wondering what to do next, when the creaking of the little wooden gate drew him to the window.

He just had time to see a man and a woman, both small and dressed in black, mounting the steps to the porch. With a sudden curiosity, which he did not attempt to master, he opened his door and listened. After a moment he heard the murmur of voices coming from the parlour, but he could distinguish nothing except Mrs. Dare's saying several times: "I'm sorry, I'm really very sorry."

The conversation went on a little longer, then the voices drew nearer and he could hear the three of them coming upstairs. Shutting his door as quietly as he had opened it, he stood there without moving. He certainly felt guilty, but continued to listen. The steps went to the end of the corridor; there was the sound of a key turning and a door opened.

Joseph went back to the window, not to see what was happening in the road, but from a belated scruple about listening; from where he now was he could hear nothing. Drops of sweat tickled his forehead, for it was hot, and he wiped his face with his handkerchief. Suddenly the houses, with their pillared porches, the sycamores bordering the brick pavements, and the sky chequered with the large yellow, purple and red leaves, the whole landscape he knew so well, appeared before him as though for the first time, with a clarity that disturbed him. He felt as though he were looking at a picture or at the back-cloth of an empty stage, waiting for someone or something to appear. At the same moment he again heard footsteps in the corridor, slower this time. A few more moments and the man in black came out of the house carrying two suitcases with Simon Demuth's initials. Joseph's throat tightened, but he did not move. He noticed that the man's overcoat was too long and flapped round his ankles and that he had a large, hooked nose, like a caricature. Behind him the woman, even smaller than he was, held a handkerchief to her face; both went back to a little car, waiting for them at the corner of the street, and in less than a minute they were gone.

IV

It was a gloomy day. At a loose end, he went for a walk in the country, but neither the blue sky nor the pleasant smell of the earth gave him peace. The path he followed slipped between the meadows to climb rather lazily up the wooded hills, and the sun-dried leaves crackled sharply under the young man's feet. He wandered about under the trees for some time, broke off a branch for a switch, then retraced his steps. On account of his new suit he did not dare run or bend down and pick up stones to throw as he would have done at home. He felt dressed up, miserable. He might as well go back to his room.

On the stairs he met Mrs. Dare with a cigarette in her hand.

"I was looking for you," she said. "Would you come here?"

When she had shut the parlour door she said suddenly in her peremptory voice: "I don't know if you've heard, Mr. Day, but Simon Demuth's parents were here just now. He's left the University."

Joseph raised his eyebrows and asked: "When is he coming back?"

She flicked the ash impatiently from her cigarette.

"He's not coming back."

After a moment she lowered her eyes and added: "I should be very much obliged if you would take his room. Yes, I had a telephone call just now. I'm expecting a visitor . . . oh, only for a few days . . . I'll explain."

Joseph's silence annoyed her and she raised her eyes. They looked at each other.

"I'll have your things moved tomorrow morning," she said. "Is that settled?"

"No," said Joseph.

Mrs. Dare opened her mouth to speak, but changed her mind. It was obvious that she had not expected a refusal. However, she decided to smile and sat down in an arm-chair, inviting Joseph to do the same. He shook his head and remained standing.

"Just as you like," she said.

Half-closing her eyes she gave him an appraising look, then drew on her cigarette.

"I like that suit," she said.

He blushed, raised his hand awkwardly to the lapel of his coat in a meaningless gesture, and let his arm fall. She laughed softly.

"You amuse me," she said.

Leaning her head against the back of the arm-chair she watched him kindly.

"That grey is rather dark; I'd have preferred something else," she went on. "I can see you in green, a deep green, but clear and sustained. Green is the right colour for red hair. Tell me, Mr. Day, is it true you want to be a clergyman?"

"No, ma'am."

"I congratulate you, you've better things to do."

He looked straight at her, his hands behind his back.

"I don't know what you mean," he said, almost inaudibly.

She put on her slyest look and, in an affected way, uttered one word: "Charming!"

During the silence that followed Joseph changed the position of his hands, clasping them in front of him. He would have gone away, but could think of no excuse for leaving. To say he had to work would be a lie. Almost in spite of himself he turned away.

"It shocks you to see me smoke," Mrs. Dare said in a more serious tone. "I know that and it pleases me. I mean, it pleases me to see you so earnest, so little spoilt by the world. Nowadays that's very rare. . . . Won't you really sit down?"

"No, thank you. I'm not tired."

She smiled again.

"What was that noise I heard last night?" she asked with studied indifference. "That heavy crash? Were you fighting?"

"No."

He hesitated, then, folding his arms defiantly, said: "My neighbours were talking very loudly and I didn't like what they were saying. I made that noise to . . ."

". . . to obtain, to impose silence?"

"Yes. I apologise."

"Oh," she replied, waving her long hand. "I wouldn't

have mentioned it if I hadn't had a letter to write, a letter to my adopted daughter . . ."

Joseph remained perfectly still.

"Moira," sighed Mrs. Dare. "Against my wishes she's leaving the school I sent her to, the third in a year. It's a long story. But she's going away in a few days, I can promise you, she and her friend Selina, who's coming with her. That girl . . ." (she made a gesture without finishing her sentence.) "Well, Moira wants her room, because it was hers before you came, you see? Anyway I'm sure you and I will come to some arrangement."

She paused for Joseph's reply, but he said nothing.

"Well, we'll talk about it again," she said carelessly, then getting up suddenly she asked: "What were your neighbours saying?"

"Well . . ."

He blushed again, taken aback by this question, which he did not know how to answer. Finally he murmured: "Improprieties."

She burst into a convulsive laugh, her shoulders and stomach shaking; her large mouth opened to show her teeth, yellow with tobacco, but there was no spark of gaiety in her pale eyes. Joseph watched her in stupefaction. When she was calmer she wiped a tear from the corner of her eye with her finger and made a sort of gurgle.

"I adore you," she said.

As the young man looked scandalised, she added: "It's only a manner of speaking, Mr. Day. I don't really adore you."

Without looking at him she passed him and went out.

Almost at once Joseph heard her laughing to herself in the corridor, repeating: "Improprieties!"

He bit his lips and went back to his room.

V

As he was leaving the dining-room that evening, he found himself face to face with Killigrew, who drew him on to the porch.

"I've something to tell you that will surprise you," he said.

He was wearing a suit of rough, strong-smelling material, with plus-fours like a golfer's and green woollen stockings. His spectacles glittered harshly in the twilight.

"Well?" said Joseph.

"Perhaps you already know what has happened to Simon?"

"Mrs. Dare told me he wasn't coming back."

Putting a hand on Joseph's shoulder, Killigrew murmured: "Joe, Simon is dead."

Joseph started, but said nothing.

"It will be better if the University doesn't know about it. His parents don't want anything said here. He and I came from the same town and I know his family. On Friday he ran away and took the train home. He was killed while handling a gun."

A short silence followed this sentence.

"A gun, why?" Joseph asked suddenly.

"Nobody knows. There's no way of finding out whether it was an accident or something else."

Joseph seized Killigrew's hand in his agitation.

123

"And you?" he said. "What do you think?"

"I don't know, I don't know anything about it," Killigrew replied gently. "My opinion is of no interest. Simon is dead."

He freed himself and went away.

VI

Joseph's first impulse was to ask David's advice, but he checked this desire and went to the library, where he spent an hour in one of the recesses, his head in his hands, his eyes fixed on a page in front of him, though he could not have said what the book was. 'Simon is dead,' he repeated, as though to force himself to believe in the truth of this statement. But it was in vain; he felt no emotion. He wished he could be moved by pity, but his eyes remained dry, and when the first shock was over his heart beat as usual. He tried to imagine Simon in his coffin, but could not. It was as though the news of this death was prowling round him, looking in vain for an opening to penetrate into his mind. Even religion gave Joseph no help, for, according to him, it was useless now to pray for Simon: Simon had been judged.

He got up, gave the book back to the librarian, and went out. Drops of rain fell on his face and he could smell the pleasant odour rising from the wet earth, faint and slightly intoxicating, and he sniffed it with enjoyment through widened nostrils. Turning up his coat collar, he went down the library steps and along the alley leading to the great avenue. Above him the wind blustered in the trees, dispersing the leaves in the dark air with a hollow noise, which sometimes stopped suddenly and at once began again. The cool evening was delicious and gave Joseph such a feeling of well-being that in spite of himself he smiled with secret happiness; his chest expanded; without realising it he walked more quickly, his hands in his pockets, and suddenly felt like running. From a habit of self-control he stopped, but he could not master, in his heart and in his whole person, an extraordinary feeling of joy, which he could not explain.

Back in his room, he threw his coat on a chair and moved several books on his table, as though he were going to work. He did in fact open his Greek grammar. He glanced over a page of declensions and frowned as he put the book down. A deep silence reigned over the house. Outside the wind was falling and in the trees the rain made a gentle, monotonous noise, like a whisper. Joseph went to the window and watched the red-brick pavement, which shone like enamel at the foot of a street lamp, while surrounding that bright spot was the night, filled with the murmur of water falling on the leaves. Once more the incomprehensible joy took hold of him; an unknown force seemed to fill his body and he suddenly put his hand on his shoulder, then on his arm, feeling his flesh, surprised at what he was doing. But almost at once he felt embarrassed and let his hand fall limply by his side.

'Simon is dead,' he thought dreamily. 'Simon does not hear the rain.' For a few seconds he saw again the little man with his sketch-book and the look in his eyes, at once anxious and imploring, like a whipped dog. "Tell me what you think of my sketches. . . ." His timid manner, that wounded look . . . One couldn't say no to him and he took advantage of it, insinuated himself. There had been that absurd affair of the flower and that shameful fit of weeping.

Suddenly Joseph put out a hand as though to brush aside the memory of these things. It was no good to think of the dead. He sat down on his bed and looked at his watch. Eleven would soon strike, but on account of the rain nothing could be heard. It was coming down harder now and he could hear the deep, liquid sound of the water rustling through the trees and the sharp drumming of the drops on the porch roof. Sometimes it was like a song, but one had to listen attentively to catch, through the general noise, the pure, distant voice in the night, which seemed to come from another world, but it was impossible to tell whether its meaning were sad or gay.

Joseph got up and put out the light. His neighbours were presumably in town, the house was so quiet, and he was glad to think he was alone. In the twilight he stretched himself, yawning with fatigue, then took off his shirt and, unbuckling his belt, slipped off his trousers. He had undressed in the dark since he was a child and always avoided looking at his body, but tonight he could not help seeing the whiteness of his limbs. Even without the light he could see the shape of his arms and his knees. His father used to say that the body led one to hell and the soul to heaven. It was true, the body was the Christian's enemy.

He put on his night-shirt and knelt down to say his prayers, but he recited them hurriedly, secretly anxious to get them over. In the middle of the Lord's Prayer he had the extraordinary idea of changing the position of his

bed, and this idea was so strong that he no longer knew
what he was saying. From a sense of duty he started
again, but again lost his place, and the next moment he
was on his feet, tugging the bed into the centre of the
room, until he had placed it obliquely at an equal distance
from the fireplace and the door. His hands shook on the
brass rail and he tore off the counterpane with a violence
which surprised himself, though since that morning he
had not been behaving normally. After walking round
the bed he stroked the pillow and sheet gently with his
finger-tips in a shy, caressing gesture. Suddenly he threw
himself on the narrow bed, whose springs groaned under
the weight of his body, and stretched out at full length.

VII

At about one o'clock in the morning he was roused from
sleep by the voice of MacAllister going back to his room
arguing with one of his friends. They had both been
drinking and Joseph gathered that they were talking about
a woman, and from habit he put his hands over his ears
and remained like that for several seconds. Suddenly
his legs relaxed and he jumped up.

"You're worse than those men!" he cried.

Standing with his hands clenched against his breast, he
repeated the phrase in a voice roughened by emotion,
panting as though he had been running. Then with a
sudden resolution he took off his night-shirt and hurriedly
dressed, not even bothering to knot his tie. Slipping his
bare feet into his shoes, he left his room and went down
to the street.

The rain had stopped. At first he strode along, then he began to run and did not stop until he had reached the house where David lodged. His first impulse was to ring at the front door, but he changed his mind on seeing that there was no light in any of the windows. He pushed open the garden gate, crossed the lawn, and went round to the back of the old house.

There the trees spread such black shadows that he had to feel along the clapboards as far as David's window. It was open, as he had expected, but the wire-screen stopped him entering the room and resisted his effort to raise it. In a low voice the young man called David and, receiving no answer, knocked on the screen with the flat of his hand and called more loudly.

The silence that followed was so deep that he did not dare break it and he remained motionless and hesitating for several minutes. The night was filled with the bitter smell of the dead leaves, and the only sound was the murmur of an intermittent breeze in the tree tops. Finally he plucked up his courage and called again.

"Is that you?" said David's voice.

"Come here," Joseph said.

In the dark he could see David's face, white behind the screen.

"Listen," he whispered, "I've been thinking. If the room is still free, I'll take it."

"You're quite right," David said in the serious tone which always grated slightly on Joseph's nerves. "I'll tell Mrs. Ferguson tomorrow."

"Aren't you surprised at my coming to see you at this time of night?" Joseph asked, unable to conquer a certain impatience.

The answer did not come at once, but finally through the screen came the words pronounced very low: "I always ask as few questions as possible."

'In other words: "I'm perfect",' thought Joseph.

He left the window, as though to go away, then suddenly came back.

"I've something else to tell you," he said with an effort.

David unhooked the screen and raised it.

"Come in," he said. "I'll light the lamp."

"No," Joseph said, "don't light it."

He hoisted himself on the window-sill and jumped down into the room.

"Sit down," said David, taking his hand to guide him to a chair.

But Joseph freed himself.

"No. I'd rather stand. Listen."

He let a moment go by, then murmured: "I'm lost, David."

These words fell into a deep silence.

"Did you hear what I just said?" Joseph asked.

"Yes," David's calm voice replied from the dark. "I assume you're speaking of the salvation of your soul?"

"Naturally."

"Only God knows if you are lost."

"I know what I am saying. I'm lost. Tonight, just now, I was sure of it. You can't imagine what wickedness and impurity there is in me. I didn't know it myself. Even a fortnight ago I didn't know it. It happened all at once. It was like a revelation and I was afraid. Yes, I thought I was just and upright before God like . . . like you, but it's not true. If you knew the thoughts that pass

129

through my mind sometimes you would never speak to me again. I lied to you. . . ."

"Be quiet," David said. "You're talking like a madman."

"Let me finish. If I were saved my life would be different; my actions prove that I'm lost. Tonight I acted like one of the damned."

"I don't want to know what you did," David broke in.

"You'll listen just the same. I'd sworn not to sleep in my bed, because of certain thoughts that came to me as I looked at it. I wanted to sleep on the floor. You see I had a presentiment of what would happen. I gave way. I . . ."

A blow on the mouth silenced him. He recoiled in astonishment.

"David!" he exclaimed.

"I had to stop you," David said.

He lit the lamp on the table. They both closed their eyes, dazzled, then re-opened them. In his blue-and-white striped pyjamas David looked more like a child than a man, and it was with a childish gesture that he brushed his long black hair off his forehead.

"Hit me if you like," he said.

Joseph shook his head.

"Do you still want to talk to me?" David said gently.

Again Joseph shook his head. What could be said in the dark could not be said in this curiously hard light, which searched his face, and his cheek still burned from the blow. He felt himself blushing with shame. It was not possible to hit David; David was David. Without saying another word, he put his hands in his pockets and left the room.

VIII

LESS than twenty-four hours later he was putting his clothes and books away in his new room under David's approving eye. Once again Joseph had given way to the reasoning of this man, whom he mentally called the parson, and his vanity suffered, but he tried not to show it. Besides, he had acted of his own free-will. He had come to see David in the middle of the night to tell him he would take the room; but in spite of this the parson had won; it always ended in the same way.

"Shall I help you?" David asked suddenly.

"No, I've finished."

He put a shirt in a drawer, a little more carefully than if he had been alone, and said: "Thank you all the same."

David rubbed his hands and smiled broadly.

"Look," he said gaily, "the sun is welcoming you."

A yellow shaft, piercing the leaves of a magnolia in front of the window, threw a patch of light about the size of a hand on the faded carpet. Joseph glanced at it, then, raising his large black eyes, looked around him. The room was low and spacious, furnished in an old-fashioned way, and had that pleasantly prim appearance still to be seen in the old houses in that district. A large bed, covered with a striped material, reared its four black wood-pillars, whose purpose was not apparent, as they supported nothing. Near the window a plain rocking-chair with a curved back looked like someone watching what went on in the street beyond the garden. In one corner an oak table stood against the wall, surmounted by an engraving of a battle in the War of Secession, showing clouds of smoke against the hills, and bearded officers in the foreground.

When he was alone Joseph listened for a moment, then a smile spread over his face: not a sound disturbed the peace of the room; he could have thought himself in the middle of the country, in spite of the little road, which was visible between the trees, and to complete the illusion the room had a faint odour of wood and fruit. He would certainly be able to work and collect his thoughts here, and if this was partly thanks to David, it was above all thanks to Him who watched so carefully over him and took him out of the company of sinners. For the last few minutes he had had the feeling that God would restore him to His friendship, that reconciliation was near, and in a burst of thankfulness he promised to spend the whole night standing, sitting, or lying on the floor in expiation of his sensual sin. His stay with Mrs. Dare now seemed like a nightmare: the obscene conversations of the students and, as an inevitable outcome, that fall from grace, which had closed the gates of Heaven. As for the disturbing, involved business of Simon, he did not like to think about it, but it was all over; he had taken leave of Mrs. Dare and was now beginning a new life of which this room was like the symbol, the sign.

"A sign," he murmured.

He could have sung aloud, run to David to embrace him, to forgive the blow of the night before, as he felt himself forgiven. Now he was sure that God loved him once more.

It was nearly half-past six when David knocked on his door and took him down to the dining-room, where

Mrs. Ferguson was waiting for them. She was small and thin and held herself very straight, as though to add to her height, and her fragile body seemed lost in a large, pleated, navy-blue cotton dress. Her hair was still black, although she was over sixty, and framed her dead-white, waxen face, clinging so closely to the bone structure that one was at once reminded of a death's head, particularly as her nose was short and narrow, and her high cheek-bones threw shadows on her hollow cheeks. But her deep-set eyes shone brightly and kindly, eloquent and smiling in a face which otherwise seemed immovable.

She gave Joseph a hand which surprised him by its lightness, and in a voice somewhat deeper than one would have expected from a woman, but firm and distinct, she said something which in his confusion he did not catch. He bowed and took the place she pointed out. Then she said a short prayer and they sat down.

The room was small and square and the table was so long that in going round it at either end one touched the walls. An oval mirror, surmounted by a copper eagle, hung above the black painted mantelpiece, and between two uncurtained windows was a portrait of a man, folding his arms across his chest in a self-confident attitude, revealing beautifully starched cuffs of a snowy whiteness. His pink, classically shaped face would have been agreeable if it had not been for the expression of the blue eyes, which seemed to wither the assembly, and although it was a bad painting, it was so conscientious and so true to life that the formidable man seemed to live and breath in his frame, ready to shoot his cuffs and make some alarming remark.

As at Mrs. Dare's, there were two silver candle-

133

sticks on the table, but here the spoons as well, though of simpler design, were of silver, not pewter. Joseph observed these details, but drew no conclusion, except that Mrs. Ferguson's austerity went hand-in-hand with a certain slightly ostentatious affluence. He did not dare open his mouth, except to eat, and was determined to model his behaviour on that of David, who said nothing.

Between these two boys in their prime of youth Mrs. Ferguson looked like an allegorical figure, there was such a contrast between her bloodless face and narrow shoulders and David's high colour and Joseph's strong frame, but none of them thought of the effect they might have on an observer. The servant who answered Mrs. Ferguson's ring after the soup turned her eyes at once towards the newcomer and seemed unable to take them away. She was a young negress with a shining, mahogany skin, and her eyes, widened by astonishment, followed him as she went round the table. Mrs. Ferguson rapidly ordered her to put down the dish and leave the room, then she started a mild conversation with her lodgers.

Joseph politely answered the questions she put to him. He was glad to be there, in that peaceful, friendly house, which had an indefinable air of dignity, and even the pepper mill, as he reached for it, had a rare and precious appearance in his simple eyes. He found no difficulty in telling the mistress of the house that he came from a very small town and that his father had formerly been an agricultural worker—which caused David some embarrassment, though Joseph did not notice it at first.

"You mean your father owned a farm," David said.

The blood rushed to Joseph's forehead and, as he

lowered his eyes, he realised how much more modest were his origins than those of the two others, who were so reserved in their manners. Through a haze he saw the pepper mill, whose fine appearance overawed him, hesitated for a moment, then in a slightly muffled voice said: "I mean my father worked in the fields."

In a dead silence he added: "Now he is blind he doesn't work."

"Blind!" Mrs. Ferguson repeated in a well-bred tone of sympathy.

She poured some water into her glass, paused, then asked Joseph what courses he was following and he satisfied her curiosity equally on this point.

"They are almost the same courses as David's," she said with an approving smile.

Dinner was soon over. As they got up from table Mrs. Ferguson asked Joseph if he smoked.

"I'm so afraid of fire," she explained.

The young man assured her that he had never smoked in his life and it seemed as though a great weight was lifted from her mind. Her affectionate glance rested on Joseph's face. She murmured: "David has told me a lot about you. I know you are not like the other boys here. You don't drink . . ."

He shook his head. Mrs. Ferguson smiled again and retired.

Alone with Joseph, David waved his hand towards the portrait.

"That's Mrs. Ferguson's husband," he explained in a low voice. "He did some excavations in Mesopotamia in 1890 and I believe he's the author of a book on Genesis, but he was a doctor by profession and very pious."

"Why does he look so bad-tempered?" Joseph asked.

"Do you think he looks bad-tempered? He has a beautiful expression, serious of course. The room you have was his. He died just before the war. Since then Mrs. Ferguson likes to have one or two students with her. It's not that she needs the money: she comes of a very good, rather rich, family, but she doesn't like being alone, you see."

"I see."

For a moment they both considered the portrait in silence, then David cleared his throat.

"You know," he said, "I owe you an apology for last night. I didn't want to hit you, but I wanted to stop you making a confession which you would afterwards have regretted and which would perhaps have given you a grievance against me."

Joseph remained motionless, still gazing at Dr. Ferguson.

"Do you understand?" David said.

"No."

"Well, there are some things better kept to oneself," David explained in his most patient voice. "You should speak about them only to God and ask his pardon, if you feel guilty. No one should stand between you and the Lord."

"Yes."

This word was followed by a silence.

"Have you forgiven me?" David whispered finally.

Joseph turned to him, his eyes shining.

"Long ago!" he cried.

Words of affection came to his lips, but he checked them. Both were silent, slightly embarrassed.

"I didn't know your father was blind," David went on. "But perhaps you don't like talking about it."

"No. I didn't think of telling you because . . ."

"I don't want to be indiscreet."

"You're not at all indiscreet. My father is very . . . irascible, even now. When he was young he used to fly into the most terrible rages and then he didn't know what he was doing. One day he quarrelled with a passing stranger because of . . . because of my mother. My father flung himself on him and would have killed him, but the other man was much stronger. He was a young Pole, who was looking for work in the district. He struck my father violently in the eyes, in both eyes, with his fists. . . ."

The blood suddenly rushed to his face and he stopped.

"It's a painful memory," David murmured. "I'm sorry I asked you."

"No," said Joseph. "On the contrary, it relieves me to confide my secrets to you. I'd rather you knew."

David smiled and they began to talk of something else. As they were leaving the dining-room and were about to say good-night, David appeared to remember an excellent piece of news that he had nearly forgotten to tell Joseph.

"By the way," he said, "I heard just now that the cafeteria opens next week."

IX

JOSEPH immediately went back to his room and studied until eleven. Then he said his prayers and undressed, as always, in the dark. Taking a blanket off the bed, he

wrapped it round him and lay on the floor with a queer
kind of satisfaction. He turned and stretched on the
boards, as though he were rolling on a feather bed, but
after a moment he lay still and waited for the sudden
plunge into sleep. But the minutes dragged by and still
he could not sleep.

'My body is uncomfortable,' he thought, 'but my soul
is at peace.' With what joy he offered to the Lord this
discomfort in his limbs. He imagined himself confessing
his faith in the midst of torment and the thought filled
him with satisfaction. He was sorry he had slipped a
dictionary under his head for a pillow, the book was too
thick and cut into his neck, but he could offer that too in
expiation, and he wondered what David would have
thought of this self-inflicted suffering. Tonight David
would sleep in his narrow but comfortable bed, and in
doing so would yield just that much to sensuality. But
then David had no sin to atone for. David never sinned.
He was undoubtedly one of the just.

He turned over, aching, on his left side. The conversation he had had with Mrs. Ferguson at dinner came back
to his mind. Perhaps he should not have told the old
lady that his father used to work in the fields. David
had not seemed very pleased, but Joseph could not help
telling the truth, even if it were embarrassing. And
David had annoyed him by mentioning the cafeteria,
particularly after Joseph had just confided in him about
his father. It did not seem the right moment. But he
forgave David, he forgave him everything, the blow and
everything else. He saw him again on his knees, the
night they had prayed together, and he could not repress
a feeling of admiration, almost of envy.

A pain in his shoulder forced him to change his position. There was no doubt of David's being saved. The letter which sealed the elect in Revelation was almost visible on his forehead. For a quarter of an hour he pondered on these matters, listening to the sounds in the old house: a light step over his head, a door closing carefully. Mrs. Ferguson's room was on the same side as David's, facing the garden behind the house, while his own room looked out on to the street. Suddenly the floor near his head creaked, as though from an invisible footstep. Joseph opened his eyes and through the darkness saw the window curtain moving gently in the breeze; he felt the cool air on his cheek, lifting the hair on his forehead. He was uncomfortable on his left side, but it reassured him to see the window and the square of white muslin, which seemed to live and breathe.

Suddenly he was seized by a great longing to be at home, in his parents' house. He remembered a bundle of maize which hung on the wall near his bed, and the bright patchwork counterpane, which his mother had made with old scraps of material, and the smell of his room came into his mind. His heart ached. He promised inwardly to write to his mother the next day, telling her, as usual, that he was well and read his Bible every day. In memory his house seemed very small, as though seen through the wrong end of a telescope. In front of it was the common, surrounded by a wooden fence, some of whose planks were so old that the rain had worn ridges in them. From the attic you could see the little grey wooden church, with its square tower, and further away still the woods, which became red after the first cold nights, and which smelt so pleasant that you wanted to lie down on the thick layer of dead leaves and stay there until evening, breathing the bitter-sweet odour rising from the ground.

Thinking of all this he felt a sadness bordering on despair and, shutting his eyes, tried again to sleep, but the pain in his shoulder kept him awake and, for a reason he would not admit, he hesitated to change his position. At least he could try and think of something else. Mrs. Ferguson's pallid face came into his mind and automatically he wondered if she were saved. He did not like to admit that it was all the same to him. In any case how did one know if a soul were saved or not? David was a special case. With the great majority of people one could not tell. Suddenly he thought of Mrs. Dare with her painted mouth and her cigarette and he opened his eyes wide, as though he had been hit. Was that woman saved? The hard, flat voice, sharp as a knife, sounded in his memory: "You're leaving, Mr. Day? Well, Moira is arriving tomorrow. She'll have her room back." Tomorrow: that was today. While he lay on the floor, Moira was asleep in her bed, the bed where he had slept for three weeks. She would be again aware of the depression which caught the small of the back, forcing her to curl her body a little to adjust it to the hollow. The girl herself had hollowed the mattress in that place, it was her flesh, the weight of her flesh.

His heart began to beat violently. It was starting again. The images came back automatically to his mind in an inexorable sequence. He had never before thought of a woman, or so fleetingly that it did not count, did not sully him, but tonight, as last night, his blood was on fire. "She's pretty, Miss Moira . . ." The old servant's

140

commonplace words came back to him adorned with extraordinary grace. In spite of himself he tried to imagine Moira; her skin should be beautiful, golden, and her bright eyes and her bosom, what one could see of her bosom, of that part of the body which is usually hidden. . . .

Suddenly he threw back the blanket and stood up. The boards creaked under his feet and he had the impression that the shadows were people. For the last half hour he had been worried, without admitting it, by the idea that he was not alone between these walls. It was not a question of ghosts—he was not affected by such stories—but of something quite different which he could not have described or even named. It was like a presence dispersed throughout the night and surrounding him like air. He picked up the blanket, threw it round his shoulders and sat down by the window in the rocking-chair, which tipped back under his weight. The street was clearly visible at the end of the garden between the trees, which were silhouetted blackly against the lighter sky; he could even see the corner of a white house and it reassured him a little. Mechanically he recited: "The Lord is my shepherd," but the words seemed to die on his lips, because something inside him contradicted them. The Lord was not his shepherd.

He shivered. The breeze was cooler now and flowed over his face and chest like water, and he drew the blanket up to his ears. His eyes, turned to the garden, half closed, but he fought against sleep. On his left was the great mass of shadow, which in some mysterious way was watching him, and he wished he had thought before of going to the door and turning on the light, instead of sitting by the window, for now he could not cross the room. He was afraid. He did not realise this at first, but from time to time he threw a furtive glance across the room and instinctively pushed his chair further to the right. After a few minutes he stopped looking at the garden and turned his head towards the door, where the shadows were thickest. 'I'm cold,' he thought, trembling, and he tried to pull the blanket more closely round him, but his hands clutching the rough material seemed to turn to marble. He tried to distinguish the columns of his bed, the square of the fireplace; his eyes met only a kind of black wall. He could just recognise part of the ceiling from its vague whiteness and he forced his attention on the cloudy patch as though on an island in the middle of the maleficent darkness. Now the impure thoughts which a short while before had been fascinating him vanished, leaving only terror, and in the confusion of his mind one thought arose more clearly, quietly at first, like someone making his way patiently through a crowd, then victoriously, triumphantly: 'You were wrong. God does not forgive so quickly. It is written that no unclean person has any inheritance in the Kingdom of God. You are lost.'

He did not move. Something deep inside him was stricken, and he cautiously held his breath, as though he hoped to conceal his presence from the enemy, but his whole body had become so heavy that he could not raise a finger. The skin above his ears and on the nape of his neck became taut, and his heart beat with the sound of a fist knocking on a thick wall. Suddenly he could no longer see the long white patch of ceiling and, like a man falling into space, he felt that all his blood was rushing upwards and that his entrails were turning over.

When he next opened his eyes he saw the door in the grey light which stealthily brushed the walls; its two panels were framed in a black line which seemed to lead the eye unceasingly from the bottom to the top and from left to right. Not without an effort he turned his head a little and saw the bed with its shining columns and the chest of drawers with its brass handles. Something took hold of his throat and he thought he was going to weep, but he controlled himself. Then a wild joy flooded him. In the trees a bird uttered a few shy notes, stopping as though afraid. Joseph recognised the song of a thrush and sighed with happiness. 'I've been asleep,' he thought 'I was dreaming.'

X

SHORTLY before breakfast David knocked at his door. A smell of soap and toothpaste surrounded him and under his long, sleek, black eyebrows his bright blue eyes shone more brilliantly than usual, as though from increased optimism.

"How did you sleep?" he asked.

Joseph felt slightly pleased at telling him that he had had rather a bad night. After all, it was thanks to David that he had this room.

The "parson's" face clouded.

"Don't you like it here?"

"I didn't say that."

David looked round him.

"I like this room. Perhaps you're not yet used to the bed. The first night . . ."

Joseph assumed a mysterious and patient expression and said nothing. David looked at him attentively.

"I'm sure something's wrong," he said.

"Well," Joseph cried, "if you must know there is something . . . it's silly. My sweater . . . I wanted to put it on this morning because I was cold. I've looked in the drawers, but it isn't there."

Averting his head slightly, he added: "I must have left it at Mrs. Dare's."

"You can't have looked properly. It's impossible."

"Why is it impossible?" Joseph asked, suddenly irritated. "It's quite easy to leave a sweater in the bottom of a drawer. It's been left in my old room. There's nothing extraordinary about it!"

"Quite. There's nothing to get excited about, either. You can go and get it between the Greek and English classes."

"I shall go when I like."

"Of course," David said with a smile. "Meanwhile, come and have breakfast."

As soon as the Greek class was over, Joseph ran to Mrs. Dare's and stopped, out of breath, in front of the house. He had the curious feeling of having left it months ago and it seemed at once new and familiar, a little uglier than he had thought, a bit more dilapidated, and in his heart he hated it.

As usual the front door was half open and he went in without ringing. In the hall the smell of cooking and dust he knew so well assailed him, and so many memories came back that for a moment he almost felt giddy. The students were at their classes and the silence of the house was broken only by the sound of washing up in the scullery. Nothing had changed and as he went up the stairs Joseph felt like a ghost, but although he walked as quietly as he could, the stairs, one after the other, made a noise like the imperious cracking of a whip. Suddenly nervous, he stopped and wondered if he would run away, when the door of his room opened.

"Is that you, Selina?" a woman's voice asked.

Joseph stood quite still. He could not be seen, for he could not see the door himself, and with his back to the wall he waited.

"Who's there?" the voice asked.

Instead of going up he went down a step and was about to give his name, but did not dare. Heels sounded loudly on the landing and the woman leant over the banisters and said: "Who's there? Will you please answer?"

He saw her. She was dressed in red, a dark but violent red which shocked him. Small and thin, she moved her narrow shoulders as she talked and metal bracelets tinkled on her impatient wrists. Her black hair, drawn back and carefully brushed, shone like jet and made a kind of helmet, showing her tiny, extraordinarily fine, ears. She was standing against the light and he could not see her face, and in any case he felt his eyes grow dim.

"Who do you want to see?" she asked.

"Nobody."

His voice was choked, but he managed to say: "I've left something in my room."

"What room? You haven't a room here as far as I know."

"My old room."

"Come on up," she said.

He obeyed. When he was before her he looked at her, then lowered his eyes in spite of himself. She was not at all like the woman he had imagined and seemed at once more attractive and less beautiful. Her face, with its high cheek-bones and flat cheeks, had a pallor tinged with purple, which brought out the lustre of her large eyes, which were the colour of the sea. The fine texture of her skin was like nothing so much as a flower, and across it an over-red mouth had been firmly, almost brutally, painted. He seemed to be looking at a mask rather than a human face.

"Which was your room?" she asked.

He gestured at the door.

"But that's my room!" the young woman exclaimed.

Suddenly she burst out laughing.

"Then you're the red-haired student!"

He looked at her, taken aback, and again lowered his eyes, this time deeply troubled.

"I was told in a letter that my room was occupied by a red-haired student, but all the same I didn't think you were that red. Look at me properly! Do I scare you?"

"No," he said, raising his eyes.

"Black eyes," she said, as though to herself. "I didn't imagine you had eyes like that. Red-heads generally . . ."

She did not finish and went back to her room, her heels clattering on the floor.

"Come on in," she commanded. "Nobody's going to eat you."

He followed her timidly into the room and he had difficulty in recognising even the furniture, which was covered with dresses, hats and boxes. A white silk blouse shamelessly opened its arms on the rocking-chair and in the middle of the unmade bed a pair of flesh-coloured stockings and a pink night-dress were thrown in a heap. He turned away, horrified. His hesitating glance next went to the mantelpiece, where perfume bottles and boxes of cosmetics were carelessly ranged. On the work-table a silver powder-box was open, showing a white, round puff, like a little cloud. Between the walls floated a shockingly sweet, intoxicating perfume, which he tried not to breath, a smell of lilac.

She began to laugh again.

"I suppose it's my untidiness that makes you pull that face? Women live in untidiness, you know that!"

With one hand on her hip she looked at him.

"Haven't you ever seen a woman's bedroom?"

He was about to say: "My mother's bedroom," but stopped just in time. Seeing he was not going to answer, she asked in her rather singing tones: "What did you leave here?"

"My sweater."

Without speaking she opened the wardrobe door and, stretching to the back, brought out a blue woollen sweater, which she threw on the floor.

"That?" she said, pushing it towards the young man with her foot. "I thought it was a rag for cleaning my shoes."

He did not move.

"Well," she said. "What are you waiting for? Pick it up and go away."

Suddenly he bent down, raging inside at this woman, and his hand clenched on the wool. As he was going to the door she stopped him.

"One moment," she said. "Look at me, please, unless I frighten you."

Against his will he turned round and fixed his eyes, large with anger, on her. The young woman pouted her full lips contemptuously.

"You have got . . ."

She left the sentence in suspense for two or three seconds, then with a half-smile finished: ". . . a queer face!"

Joseph's cheeks and ears burned and after a moment's hesitation he went out. On the staircase he heard the young woman's voice, which seemed to follow him from stair to stair.

"You didn't tell me your name."

Without answering he went on down. She walked to the banisters with queenly indifference.

"Good-bye, baby!" she said.

These words, uttered in a winning tone, reached him as he was crossing the threshold of the house and he felt like slamming the door. He managed to control himself and shut it as gently as he could, but his large white hand held the brass handle so tightly that for a long time afterwards he had the impession of still holding it in his palm.

XI

HALF AN HOUR later he entered the big bare lecture-hall, where the students were reluctantly taking their places. There were about sixty of them, dragging their feet and wearing an expression of gloomy apathy, which contrasted with their professor's countenance, shining with optimism. A spare, upright little man, whose pale grey suit had a touch of elegance, he stood up on the platform with his hands on his desk, waiting for silence, while the sun, catching his gold-mounted pince-nez, gave a fiery look to his white, freckled face.

It was only the second time Joseph had been in this hall since he changed courses and he could not find his place. He sat down at random next to a student whom in his confusion he did not recognise, but who at once got up and went to the back of the class. There was a moment's commotion, then the empty place next to Joseph was taken by a stocky, laughing boy, who nudged his neighbour with his elbow.

"You're in my place," he said. "It doesn't matter, but now I'm in Praileau's."

At this name Joseph turned and stared at the boy, who replied by squinting horribly. He had a round, child-like face with a snub nose covered with freckles.

"Why do you make that face?" Joseph asked.

"I squint from birth. We all squint in our family. And we're a bit hunchbacked too."

He hitched one shoulder up to his ear and rolled the whites of his eyes. Joseph turned his head away. A violent nudge made him start.

"What's your name?" his neighbour asked.

"Joseph Day."

"Oh? Mine's Terence MacFadden, like the fellow in the song who wanted to learn dancing, but I answer to the name of Terry."

This conversation was interrupted by the clear, nasal voice of the professor, who was continuing his lectures on Chaucer and he read the Prologue to the *Canterbury Tales*, emphasising the Norman vowels. Frown as he might, Joseph could not follow this artless, mocking story, which still had the pungency of French speech, and he was again anxious on realising that he did not understand, that even the words of his own language escaped him. Perhaps, too, he was too upset to follow the thread of the old poem. In spite of himself his memory retraced all the circumstances of his meeting with Moira. So that was what she looked like—this small, proud, insolent woman . . . He had pictured her quite differently and the real Moira seemed if not ugly at least too odd, too foreign in appearance for him to admire her. Foreign, that was it. A woman from a distant country. Dressed in red, like the whore in Revelation, her lips painted. He saw himself stooping before her to pick up his sweater. What joy it would have given him to rub her mouth with the rough wool, what dreadful joy to strike and punish, yes punish, her for her arrogance! The blood rushed to his head.

He made an effort to calm himself, to listen to the verses whose even beat resembled the tranquil progress of a cart-horse, and little by little his anger fell. At heart he was somewhat relieved at the thought that Moira was not as he had seen her in his impure dreams. It was better that way. God had not allowed it. A fragment of a psalm came into his mind: 'God, the rock of my salvation . . .' and his heart swelled, while sentences from the Bible began to beat their wings around him, like great birds stirring the air with their gigantic feathers. What sense could these useless verses have when measured against such words? He paid attention only from a sense of duty and because he had to learn. Folding his arms, he listened.

How was it he had not noticed Praileau in the hall on the first day? The question nagged at his mind. But so many students followed a course known to be easy that he might quite well have gone unnoticed. Besides, what did he care if Praileau were there or not? But for all that he felt uncomfortable and several times looked furtively over his shoulder. Next time he would sit as far away as possible at the other end of the class, for he felt that he was being looked at, that everyone was looking at him on account of his red hair. With a gesture of vanity, of which he was utterly unconscious, he ran his hand over his hair and again folding his arms in a manly attitude threw out his chest like a soldier.

Suddenly a few lines of extreme simplicity caught his ear. They were about a young bachelor going to Canterbury on horseback, and the poet, in words seemingly borrowed from the language of childhood, showed him in a garment "embroidered as it were a mede", his head curled, full of elegance and as fresh, added the old author, as is the month of May.

"Short was his goune, with sleeves long and wyde.
Wel cowde he sitte on hors, and faire ryde.
He cowde songes wel make and endite,
Justne and eek daunce and wel purtray and write.
So hote he lovede, that by nightertale
He sleep nomore than doth a nightyngale."

Joseph opened his mouth in surprise. He had not expected the last two lines, which made him blush without quite knowing why. 'That's poetry,' he thought vaguely.

'In poetry people never sleep when they're in love.' But the word love shook him and still more the qualifying word preceding it—so hot he loved. One should not say such things, far less write them. Was he going to have the same difficulty with Chaucer as with Shakespeare? He glanced round him; his companions were listening attentively and he noticed a smile dimpling his neighbour's round cheeks. How could they be interested in such nonsense? But their heads were full of impurity, and the moment anyone mentioned love they became like animals. Did they never think of the flames that were waiting to prey on them?

In a charitable impulse he leant towards Terence MacFadden and whispered in his ear: "You'd better not listen!"

"Yes, I'm listening," MacFadden whispered back, mishearing him. "You'll see a bit later on there's the Wife of Bath. It's a scream. I read it yesterday."

With his chin on his fists he gazed at the pale face uttering the sensuous words. Joseph looked at him in silence and his heart contracted in pity. Yielding to a sudden impulse he scribbled on a piece of paper, which he passed to MacFadden: "Are you a Christian?"

At first the recipient of this message did not notice it and Joseph had to touch his elbow and point to the paper. Terence MacFadden frowned, then raising his clear eyes looked straight at Joseph.

"Of course," he whispered.

And he added: "You don't happen to be ill, do you?"

With a shrug he resumed his studious attitude, but his snub profile betrayed a certain bad temper, and one might almost have said that his nose curled with anger.

Joseph thought for a moment, then on another piece of paper wrote: "Presbyterian, Methodist or Baptist?"

This time he folded the paper twice and put it in front of his neighbour, right between his elbows. MacFadden pretended not to see it at first, but, overcome by curiosity, he unfolded the note. Two deep parallel lines marked his narrow, low forehead. In a hand shaking with exasperation he wrote on the same paper: "Roman Catholic." Then he turned his attention angrily back to the professor.

Joseph recoiled slightly. Where he came from there were no Catholics and he never thought about them, except when reading those passages in the prophecies where the Church of Rome was clearly indicated in the form of the woman clothed in scarlet and the great whore of Babylon, but now God had allowed, had wished him to be seated next to one of the children of the abyss, for as surely as the sun shone through the tall windows, spilling great pools of golden light on the floor of that hall, Terence MacFadden was lost, the Kingdom of Heaven being closed for ever against idolaters.

The thought that he was breathing the same air as one of the damned suddenly came to him and gave him a kind of horror mingled with passionate interest. From time to time he glanced at his neighbour and, seeing him so calm, so careless of the destiny weighing on him, Joseph was moved with an obscure and violent compassion. Meanwhile the idolater was smiling like a child at the poet's old-fashioned pleasantries and between his full lips a row of irregular teeth showed like the teeth of an ogre.

THE next few weeks went by without incident and Joseph experienced an inner peace which reminded him of happier days before he had known the temptations of the flesh. It seemed that everything had begun on his coming there and hearing the boys talk about their women; and then there was Moira . . . But things were better now. He felt somehow sheltered at Mrs. Ferguson's, where he was left alone, and he was becoming used to his room; then he was glad David was there, near him, for David was so reasonable. And if Joseph sometimes thought of Moira it was to tell himself that after all she in no way resembled the woman of his imagination. This reassured him. In one way it could be said that Moira revolted him: he remembered that she had been wearing a tight-fitting dress that clearly outlined some parts of her body, and the fact that the dress was red had aggravated the indecency.

Something prevented his talking to David about his encounter with the young woman and he merely said that he had found his sweater. On the other hand, driven by a perpetual desire to confide in someone, he told him one day about the exchange of notes in the English class with Terence MacFadden.

"I think you were wrong," David said. "One shouldn't ask strangers such personal questions."

"But perhaps I would never have known otherwise that he was a Catholic."

"And where does it get you to know that he's a Catholic? Besides, with a name like his he couldn't be anything else," he added with a smile.

Joseph bit back the words that rose to his lips. Too many thoughts agitated him for him to be able to express them clearly.

"Come with me," David said, "and make a tour of the garden. I don't think we've ever been there together. And I have something to tell you."

They left the house by the back door and took a little path hedged with privet, which was soon lost among the elms and sycamores. The thick layer of dead leaves parted under their feet with the sound of a waterfall, almost drowning their voices, and they walked on until they reached a black wooden shed against a low wall, whose red bricks were turning purple in places.

"They keep the garden tools here," David explained, opening the door. "Some years ago they found a rattlesnake behind the hose, which is why Mrs. Ferguson had the wall built. You can step over it, but it stops snakes coming into the garden."

Joseph craned his neck and saw the rakes, spades and the hose David had mentioned inside the shed. Beyond the little wall a piece of waste land covered with rusty bushes stretched as far as the railway embankment, which formed an endless line across the pale blue sky, a hard, clear blue, foretelling winter.

"I want to tell you a secret," David said with somewhat theatrical suddenness. "You're my friend and should know. I'm engaged."

Joseph looked at him.

"Engaged!" he repeated, stupefied.

"Yes. To a girl at home. We came to an understanding six months ago. Would you like to see her photograph?"

Without waiting for a reply, he took from his wallet a photograph of a young girl, small with a pleasant, round face, dimpled arms and a submissive smile.

"Don't you think she's pretty?" David asked.

He added immediately: "I must say that the photograph doesn't flatter her. Her colouring is lovely. She is an angel, an angel sent from God. We shall be married as soon as I take orders."

He smiled broadly and said in a gay, almost teasing, voice: "I bet you're envious!"

At these words Joseph seized both David's arms, as though to immobilise him, and looking into his face said slowly: "Believe me, David, I am not. Marriage is a dangerous temptation."

"What do you mean?"

"You know very well what I mean," Joseph answered, his eyes glittering. "The flesh, the pleasures of the flesh and all the impurity implicit in them."

"Be quiet!" David cried, freeing himself.

"When you hold that woman in your arms will you think of God?"

David did not answer, but, red with anger, turned aside his face and walked away. Joseph folded his arm like a conqueror and quoted in a clear, calm voice: "No fornicator hath any inheritance in the kingdom of Christ and God."

There was a silence. David let one or two minutes go by, then came back to his friend.

"Joseph," he said with a smile, "we won't talk any more about my plans for the future. You were offensive, but I don't think you meant to be."

"I've warned you. God has cursed fornicators."

"Let's take it that you've warned me. We must not let the sun go down on our anger. Give me your hand. I have never committed the sin you speak of. And you forget that St. Paul said that it is better to marry than to burn. Give me your hand, Joseph."

After a moment's hesitation Joseph held out his hand defiantly. Once more David had the star part; it nearly always ended in the same way. They shook hands and went back to the house in silence, the only sound being the loud rustle of the dead leaves. As they went up the steps David stopped and said: "These words . . . fornicator and fornication that you're so fond of using are rather harsh and unpleasant. I know they're to be found in the Bible, but in spite of that we ought to use them with discernment, don't you think?"

Joseph did not reply.

"May I say something for your good, yes, for your good," David went on. "I'll admit I'm reluctant to say it, and I won't if you forbid me."

He waited for a few seconds, then holding Joseph's arm tightly stammered in an embarrassed voice: "Forgive me for what I'm going to say, Joseph, but you think too much about . . . fornication, about what you call fornication. You shun it, I know, but you think about it."

"I think about it as one thinks about something one loathes," Joseph said hoarsely.

David raised anxious eyes.

"Joseph," he said, "one should never think about it at all."

This was said with such serious emphasis that Joseph felt his throat contract.

"I can't help it," he breathed.

XIII

HE went and shut himself up in his room. He was so agitated by his conversation with David that he had to lie down on the bed to recover, but the memory of his own final words disturbed him much more than his friend's admonitions. Was it true that he could not help thinking about fornication? Why had he said that? He debated these questions in his mind for several minutes, then, turning over suddenly, hid his face in his arms. A voice, made gentler by suffering, rose in the silent room, which seemed to listen: 'My God, give me a pure heart!'

But was there a pure heart on the whole earth? Did not David himself think of the works of the flesh? The thought brushed his mind that almost all humanity was lost: the moment the senses were awakened the devil resumed his rights; only children and a few saints would see God in Paradise; the rest would burn ceaselessly, burn for ever.

Leaving his bed, he went to the window and with an unconscious gesture raised his hand to his breast. 'The saints,' he thought. There had been some saints in the Bible, perhaps there were some now, and he had certainly thought David was one, but this marriage scheme did not fit in with Joseph's conception of the elect, the man predestined to glory. He remembered the words of the Lord to the unfaithful church: 'Thou hast left thy first love . . . I will remove thy candle-stick out of his place . . . ' Perhaps the grace formerly bestowed on David would be given to another. His heart beat rapidly. How mysterious the whole room suddenly seemed. It was as though the partition between the visible and invisible worlds had become thinner. Nothing had changed, and yet nothing had its familiar appearance. Even the light seemed to come from elsewhere than the sky, fiery with the dusk.

He stood quite still for some time, as though afraid that a movement might interfere with some unknown law and, without knowing why, he felt intensely happy. Words came to his mind with a curious persistence: 'A stranger in the land,' but their sound did not sadden him; on the contrary, they filled him gradually with an ineffable sweetness.

Night fell almost at once and Joseph groped for the lamp on his table. He felt as though he were awaking from a strange dream through which he had seen the reverse side of the world—like going behind a piece of scenery—and he needed time to fall into his habitual gestures, to put out his books on the table and, when he had opened them, to understand what he saw there. From all this vague ecstasy there remained only a faint excitement, which soon passed away, in spite of his efforts to retain it, for it was pleasant, and yet a quarter of an hour later, absorbed by an exercise in Greek grammar, he was thinking only of the conjugation of verbs in $\mu\iota$.

It was not without annoyance that he heard a knock at the door and at first he was tempted not to answer. Grudgingly he said: "Come in!"

Killigrew appeared in a green suit with plus-fours falling over thick-ribbed woollen stockings. He looked like a tourist or a golfer, but his face was serious and his mouth harder than usual.

"Hello, Joe," he said in his colourless, nasal voice.

"I hope I'm not disturbing you. Mrs. Dare gave me your address."

He glanced round, then sat down in the arm-chair.

"Nice room," he said, rocking himself.

With folded arms, Joseph looked at him in silence.

"Do you mind if I smoke?" Killigrew asked, taking a long jade-green cigarette holder from his pocket. Without waiting for a reply he explained: "It steadies my nerves. You must forgive me."

Lighting his cigarette, he began: "I've come to talk to you about various people, principally about yourself, about Simon, and about . . ."

"I don't want to talk about Simon," Joseph said in a low voice.

"You've never wondered about him at all?"

"No, never. I hardly knew him."

Killigrew inclined his head slightly and looked at Joseph more attentively.

"Well, we won't talk about Simon," he said slowly. "But Simon was right: there are some things one would never say in your presence simply because one couldn't. You intimidated him. You don't intimidate me, but . . . I can understand his keeping silence."

A short pause followed these words, then he went on: "You are so . . ."

He hesitated, smiled, drew on his cigarette and said finally: ". . . virginal!"

Joseph reddened.

"It's ridiculous," he murmured. "What you're saying is ridiculous."

But Killigrew went on with the gentle care one uses in speaking to invalids.

"The word should not shock you. I can well believe, though, that it disturbs you, because it concerns something that worries you, I should say that appals you."

"I don't understand," Joseph said.

"There is a part of yourself that horrifies you."

"A part of myself," Joseph repeated.

"Your body," Killigrew said in an altered voice.

They were again silent. The visitor had suddenly become very pale and looked fixedly at Joseph, who averted his head violently. After a moment Killigrew went on: "You can see nothing but an enemy in your body. You imagine it comes to you from the Devil. All flesh is accursed in your eyes."

He became animated, and put down his holder on the window-sill.

"We're living in 1920, Joe. Your ideas are from another age. You must wake up, get out of yourself, hear what's said around you."

Joseph looked at him.

"I've heard more than once," he said. "I've listened in spite of myself. I've listened to you talking with MacAllister and the others. It was horrible."

"I don't know what you could have heard. No doubt we were talking freely among ourselves, as men do. Perhaps it was about physical love. Men of our age think of nothing else, Joe. It's quite natural."

A cunning smile appeared on his face. Leaning forward a little, he added: "You yourself, Joe, think of it perhaps."

Leaving his chair, Joseph clasped his hands behind his back and flashed an angry look at his visitor.

"Leave me alone, Killigrew," he said.

"I don't want to irritate you," Killigrew replied humbly, "I came with good intentions. You'd be surprised to know to what extent . . ."

He stopped and, faced with Joseph's silence, went on: "You could make a good many friends at the University. I don't want to be fulsome, but . . ."

He rocked himself gently and murmured: "You've got everything."

For a few seconds the only sound was the creaking of the floor under the rocking-chair, then Killigrew's voice was heard again, timidly this time.

"Hasn't anyone ever told you?"

Joseph did not move. Moira's words came back to his mind: 'You have got a queer face!'

"No," he said violently. "All I know is that I've got a queer face. And that's what I've been told."

"What!" cried Killigrew. "What man was blind enough, or stupid enough . . ."

"Oh, it wasn't a man! Besides, I don't care."

"A woman told you that?"

"Yes, a woman."

At these words Killigrew's face seemed to harden into stone and his eyes became quite small.

"What woman?" he asked.

"That's none of your business."

"You're wrong, Joe. It's the main reason for my coming. I've come to do you a favour and to put you on guard."

"I don't understand you."

"Without revealing the name of this woman you can at least tell me if it's a woman from here."

"Well, yes."

Killigrew leaned back in his chair.

"Say no more," he remarked with a smile. "I perfectly recognise the style of the person in question."

His eyes on the window, Joseph said nothing.

"It's Moira," said Killigrew. "I know she's seen you, because she told MacAllister, and anyway you don't know any women here. I except your present landlady and Mrs. Dare, because neither of them would have spoken to you like that. There remains Moira. Am I right?"

Joseph bit his lips.

"Of course it's Moira," Killigrew resumed, rocking. "But let me tell you that the opinion of this . . . woman has not the slightest value. She'd give herself to a gorilla if a gorilla made love to her. The whole point is that you don't make love to her and that annoys her. One can't count the number of boys who've had what they wanted from her. She was sent away from her school for misconduct and she's come back here because she likes some of the students. She was supposed to be staying for three days, it seems. Three days! She hasn't the slightest intention of leaving. She's what the Romans called *lupa*, a wolf, a beast perpetually famished . . ."

"I don't like what you're saying," Joseph said without moving.

"Can you deny that she dresses in a provocative way, that she paints like one of those women who ought to horrify you? There's a disreputable atmosphere round her, the kind you get in certain houses. I don't want to moralise. It would be ridiculous coming from me. But really she is rather . . . repulsive. And, who knows? Dangerous."

163

"Dangerous?"

"Yes, Joe. You are appallingly innocent. All the same, someone must have told you that some women are dangerous."

"I know," Joseph said suddenly, "I've been told."

"Besides," Killigrew went on, "this conversation disposes of my last scruples. I know I'd promised to say nothing, but there's a plot against you."

"Against me?"

"Oh, don't let's exaggerate: a little plot, a students' bad joke. Last week they swore to make little Stuart, who is so shy, lose his innocence. You must have seen him at Mrs. Dare's. They made him drunk and took him into town, practically by force. There, in front of their eyes, he committed a certain act with a woman. Do you understand?"

"I understand."

"They want to play a trick on you as well. I don't say the same trick, but . . ."

"Well?" Joseph asked, all at once very calm.

"Well, you must be careful. Your rather fanatical morality exasperates them. They'd like to see you in a ridiculous situation, one harmful to your reputation."

"God will punish them," Joseph said gently.

"In any case I thought I'd warn you."

Joseph did not reply. Standing some way away from Killigrew, who rocked and watched him, he looked through the window into the distance, as though seeking some answer from the depths of the sky; an indescribable sadness spread over his features, from one part of his face to another—first the eyes and then the mouth.

At this moment there was a quiet knock at the door

and as though wakened from a dream Joseph cried: "Come in!"

The door opened to admit an old negress dressed in black and wearing a white apron reaching to her feet. Her lips and eyelids seemed purple against her ebony face and the wrinkles in her cheeks and forehead might have been drawn in ink. A pair of steel-rimmed spectacles gave her a wise, austere appearance, and in her outstretched arms she was carrying a large, grey woollen blanket, folded in four.

"Mrs. Ferguson says you will need an extra blanket," she said, putting her burden down on the bed.

She glanced at Joseph, who remained motionless and did not utter a sound.

"The nights are getting much colder," Killigrew remarked.

Leaving his chair, he went to the bed and pretended to feel the blanket, as though it had been for his own bed.

"How thick it is!" he said with an approving smile. "It must be very warm."

"It's certainly very heavy to carry," said the maid as she left the room.

When she had shut the door Killigrew took a few steps towards Joseph, looking at him uncertainly.

"You didn't say anything," he said, "so I talked instead."

Joseph did not reply.

"Why do you look so serious?" asked Killigrew softly "You are so unsociable."

And in a tone half-way between complicity and pleading he added: "Who knows? We could be friends if you liked."

He put out his hand cautiously until it rested lightly on Joseph's, making him start. Their eyes met.

"Why do you touch me?" Joseph cried, clenching his fist.

Killigrew became livid and his eyes wavered behind his glasses; he opened his mouth to speak, but no sound came out; his hand fell.

"Get out!" Joseph ordered.

XIV

A FEW days later, as Joseph and David were going to a class, they passed Moira in the long avenue. She was wrapped up in a navy-blue coat, which showed her slender but strong legs; her excessively high heels tapped impatiently on the pavement. Joseph turned his head away, but out of the corner of his eye he caught the contemptuous glance she directed at him and the blood rushed to his face.

When they had gone some way under the sycamores, where curved branches still bore a few yellow leaves, Joseph said suddenly: "That was Mrs. Dare's adopted daughter we just passed. Her name is Moira."

He paused for a moment, secretly hoping that David would question him. Finally he went on: "I happened to speak to her one day."

"In that case," David said tranquilly, "I think if I'd been you I would have said good-morning."

"I purposely didn't; I didn't want to."

This declaration was met by a profound silence, but Joseph seemed relieved by what he had said and the two young men spoke no more until they had reached the arcade by the side of the big lawn. Then Joseph spoke again.

"David," he said, "I'm going to try and convert Terence."

"Terence?"

"Yes, Terence MacFadden, the Catholic I told you about the other day. Last night I felt sure that God wishes me to save him."

He expected an outburst, perhaps even an exclamation of enthusiasm, and looked at his friend, but David's wise, regular profile showed no emotion.

"If I might advise you," David said at last, "I should act with discretion. You don't know anything about Catholics. You'd better leave this one alone."

"But I can't see him heading for disaster and do nothing."

"Nobody can possibly say for certain that he's heading for disaster. You've been taught, as I have, that to be saved it is enough to be baptised and to believe in Christ. If Terence MacFadden fulfils these two conditions, he will go to Heaven."

"David!" cried Joseph, stopping. "Do you really believe what you've just said?"

David stopped too and looked at Joseph with his calm eyes.

"Without the shadow of a doubt."

They went on. Joseph's head was sunk on his chest as he pondered. The evil was greater than he had feared. It was this scheme of marriage which blinded David. Corruption already had a hold on him, but he would save him, he would save them all. With a sudden affectionate impulse he put his arm round his companion's shoulders and in a voice that rose slightly, he said: "Do you believe that we are saved, David, both of us?"

"Yes," said David, "but you ask yourself too many questions."

They had left the long arcade and were in a large open space, where the sound of their voices was lost in the pure, cold air. A neo-classical building blocked the view on one side, but on their right the blue hills could be seen between the trees splashed with yellow. Joseph's heart leaped at the sight.

"Sometimes I would like to die at once so that I could go to Heaven," he said softly, his eyes on the sky.

David began to laugh.

"What a child you are, Joseph."

The bell rang, marking the end of a class, and the students crossed the lawn, first singly, then in groups, and soon they seemed to be coming from all directions. The older ones could be recognised by their rather lazy walk and the first-year students by their haste and their serious expression. David and Joseph walked more quickly, trying to keep out of the crowd.

"I want to ask you something," Joseph said as they neared the building where the Greek class was to be held. "The woman we passed just now, Moira Dare . . ."

"Well?"

"She's not at all beautiful, is she?"

"I don't know."

"Didn't you see how she was painted. Her mouth . . ."

David looked straight at Joseph.

"I never look at women in the street," he said.

Joseph bit his lips and did not reply.

In silence they went up the steps to the peristyle and Joseph was just going to push the door when it was opened from inside and he nearly knocked into Praileau, who was coming out. The blood mounted in the latter's bronzed face and made his black eyes seem even brighter. In spite of the cold his shirt was open at the neck with elaborate carelessness and there was a hint of defiance in the way he straightened his shoulders and threw back his head. Yet he almost turned back on seeing Joseph, but pulling himself together he passed him, fixing his eyes on the library clock at the other end of the lawn. Joseph could not help turning his head and following Praileau with his eyes. 'She wouldn't have dared speak to him as she did to me when I went to get my sweater,' he thought. 'And he would never have stooped before her.' A wave of anger made him clench his teeth at the memory of the humiliations he had endured since he came to the University, and he frowned.

"What's the matter?" David enquired. "You look very worried all of a sudden."

They were passing the plaster statues and Joseph automatically lowered his eyes.

"Nothing," he said hoarsely. "Don't bother about me."

XV

As he was dressing the next morning, one of the pockets of his coat caught in the key of a drawer and was almost torn off. This accident dismayed him; he nearly went to ask David's advice, but changed his mind quickly; the only thing to do was to wear his new suit. David would probably not think so and he would have some other, eminently reasonable, solution, but this time Joseph was determined to go his own way, and three minutes later he left his room in his Sunday suit.

To his great surprise his friend appeared not to notice anything out of the ordinary and they breakfasted alone, as usual, under the gaze of Mrs. Ferguson's late husband. She herself did not get up until later. The sun sparkled on the imposing silver coffee pot and on David's hands as he dug into his grapefruit with a little spoon, taking care not to miss any of it.

"If you agree," he said without looking up, "you could come with me to the cafeteria the day after tomorrow."

'My suit has reminded him that I owe him twenty dollars,' Joseph thought. 'He's seen it all right, but he doesn't want to say anything.'

If only he had the twenty dollars on the table in silver coins so that he could give them to David and get rid of him and his cafeteria! He clasped his hands under the table and cracked his joints, as though venting his dissatisfaction on them.

"Did you hear what I said?" David asked, putting down his spoon.

"Yes, of course."

"And is that settled?"

The red head nodded, rather sharply. In silence they ate some hot bread, which steamed as they broke it, and after a few minutes, wishing to defy the young "parson", Joseph said hurriedly: "You haven't noticed that I'm wearing my new suit."

"Yes, I have," said David, pouring him out some coffee.

"Don't you want to know why?"

David filled his own cup and stirred it.

"I always ask as few questions as possible," he said gently.

"Oh," Joseph said with a smile, "I always forget that you're faultless."

David did not take up this remark, but as they were leaving the dining-room he took Joseph's arm and said: "Yesterday was my birthday. My parents sent me a present. Will you promise to say yes to the question I'm going to ask you?"

"No," said Joseph, astonished. "At least, it depends."

"Will you promise at any rate to think about it and not to say no at once."

"All right."

"I want to cancel the little debt you've incurred to me. Will you let me? No, don't answer at once."

Joseph reddened.

"If we do this," David said, giving him no time to speak, "all the money you earn at the cafeteria will be your own. I couldn't bear to think of your working just to pay me back. Anyway I shall take it that you've said yes, because you would offend me by saying no, and you know that sometimes it is as generous to receive as to give. Let's go."

As he spoke he pushed Joseph towards the door, like a grown-up pushing a child.

XVI

WHEN he was alone in his room Joseph picked up his Greek grammar and hurled it violently to the ground.

"I won't have it!" he cried.

But it was no use his saying that, he was always defeated by David. David never made a mistake, he behaved like one of the elect and, to crown everything, he could obviously read Joseph's thoughts. There were moments when Joseph detested him: his voice, his eyes, his hair, his way of eating his grapefruit with finicking gestures, in fact everything which made David David. Particularly this morning. This present wrapped up in a little sermon was the last straw. But he would not accept it. He was already turning over in his mind the words he would say that very evening: 'If I have to wear my fingers to the bone washing dishes . . .' But the words sounded silly and he would not say them, he knew very well he would not say them and that, on the contrary, he would ask David's pardon for what he had said just now and the night before. That was why he had thrown his Greek grammar on the floor and was now stamping on it, but after a moment he picked it up, ashamed, wiped it with his sleeve and passed his hands over the covers of the book, as though to console it for the treatment it had just received.

In the hall he found David waiting for him to go to the nine o'clock class.

XVII

It was always cosy in David's room. On entering one was surrounded by an exquisite warmth, as by an impalpable garment, which brought a smile of pleasure. The lamp on the table spread its peaceful light, painting a large yellow circle on the ceiling; and David looked so wise among his books that one could not imagine anything upsetting him. By day or by night he gave the curious impression of being unassailable. Joseph felt this, and sometimes it irritated him violently, but at other times his conversations with David inspired him with a feeling of inner joy.

They had been silent for a moment, both greatly moved. At last David stretched over his table and touched Joseph's hand.

"You must never speak to me like that again," he said, smiling, "never ask my pardon again. It makes me want to die of shame."

Withdrawing his hand, he added in a lower tone: "I'm too fond of you for you ever to be able really to offend me, do you understand? I'd have already forgotten what you said to me yesterday down by the shed about marriage if you hadn't mentioned it this evening."

Joseph looked at him in silence.

"Do you remember that passage of St. Paul about marriage that I quoted to you?" David went on.

"It is better to marry than to burn," Joseph quoted.

David nodded.

"That applies to us all," he said, "and to me as well as to others."

"To you!" Joseph exclaimed. "It's not possible. Are you too sometimes tempted?"

David shrugged his shoulders slightly.

"Do you think we're made of different clay?" he asked.

There was a silence, then Joseph murmured: "Is that why you're getting married?"

"I'm getting married because I'm . . . in love," David said, somewhat embarrassed.

Joseph blushed violently and lowered his eyes. He wished David had not used that dubious word which seemed to hide a sin. One could, of course, refer to the love of the saints for their wives: in the Old Testament Jacob wept with tenderness at the sight of Rachel, and in the New Testament there were Peter and his wife. But John was not married. He had better not re-open the debate, not this evening in any case. This evening he felt very close to David, in spite of this mysterious and rather painful topic. After a moment's reflection he said hesitatingly: "I want to ask you something, but it's difficult. It seems to me, indeed, that one should not think of it. And yet I want to know."

"What is it about?"

"In the desert Christ was tempted by hunger. His temptation was hunger, bodily hunger . . ."

"Yes," said David, knowing what was coming.

"And the other hunger, David. Do you know if he experienced that?"

David's eyes widened, as though in sudden fear.

"I don't know," he whispered. "I've never thought of it. It's better not to think of that, Joseph. It almost seems like blasphemy."

"I don't want to blaspheme," said Joseph in a low voice, "but I feel that if someone told me that he had suffered in that way as well I should feel stronger, I should tell myself: 'He, too . . .'"

"I don't know."

They were silent. The blood had left David's cheeks and he lowered his eyes to hide his confusion. For the space of a minute he remained completely still, then he appeared to pull himself together and said: "I worry about you sometimes. It's because I'm so fond of you. It seems to me that you tend to carry your virtues to extremes."

"What do you mean?"

"Well, the other evening Killigrew came to see me. I didn't know him before. He was talking about you."

"I don't like that man," Joseph said grimly.

"Truth compels me to say that he doesn't attract me very much either, and in fact it would be much better if you didn't talk to him."

"Talk to him! But he revolts me. There's something revolting about him. When he looks at people one has the impression he's touching them. I'm sure he is damned and that he runs after women."

"No," said David gravely, "he doesn't run after women. But that's not the point. Killigrew told me about the conversation he had with you the day you tore up your Shakespeare."

"Well?"

"Well, your prejudice against that poet is explained by your religious upbringing. But you must read him."

"Oh no, I wont!"

"Listen," said David, "we didn't meet by chance. God wants us to help one another. If you want to work to extend his Kingdom you must start preparing now, studying . . ."

"But I do study!"

". . . learning, learning as much as possible, so as to speak on equal terms with anybody, with the well-educated unbelievers you will have to save. Otherwise no one will respect you. No one will ever listen to you. Now, a man who has not read Shakespeare is an uncultured man."

Joseph lowered his head.

"You didn't read what I did in *Romeo and Juliet*."

"I'm coming to that. Some time ago I mentioned an expurgated edition of Shakespeare's plays. You're not the first person to have been shocked by lines such as you mention. There is an edition of Shakespeare from which these passages have been excluded. A man called Bowdler undertook this in the last century and has given us a perfectly harmless Shakespeare. The little volume I have here contains summaries and extracts from the most famous tragedies: *Hamlet, Othello, Antony and Cleopatra.* You must know them, in this way at least."

"Do you think so?"

"Of course. If only to learn about the human heart."

"The human heart? Do you really think so?"

"Certainly. We're eighteen, Joseph. We're no longer children. Here, look."

As he spoke he opened a drawer in his table and took out a small, thick book, which he placed before Joseph.

"I got it the other day as a present for you," he said with a shy smile. "Read what I've written on the fly-leaf."

Joseph obeyed. Above his name David had written his own with the date: November 20, 1920.

He smiled as well and did not know what to say; perhaps he was too moved.

"Thank you," he said. "I shall read this book, since you think it may be useful to me."

"I would have liked to add a verse of Scripture," David said, "but it seemed difficult to quote Scripture on the page of a secular book. Besides, what should I put?"

"Something about the human heart," Joseph suggested. "I think it would be better if there were a sentence from the Bible."

David took up his pen and considered. Suddenly Joseph exclaimed: "If our heart condemn us God is greater than our heart!"

His face took on an exalted expression and he repeated the line from the Bible in a strangled voice.

"That's it," said David, "but what's the matter with you?"

"I don't know. This verse came to my lips of its own accord. Does your heart never condemn you, David? It seems as if mine condemned me every day since I've been at the University and these words are an answer."

"Shall I write this sentence?"

"It is God Himself speaking," Joseph said, not hearing. "It is as though He had entered this room with these words in His mouth. It's enough to make one die of fear, or of joy, David. The Almighty comes to us and tells us this to reclaim us and to save us, just when we are stumbling and slipping into despair."

"Into despair?" David repeated, still holding the pen. "What do you mean?"

"You could never understand," Joseph said with heat, "because your heart does not condemn you. You are one of the just, David. I am not. You may say you are tempted, but I do not believe you. I thought evil of you, I imagined that you saw in marriage only the satisfaction of your sensual hunger, because I thought you were like myself. No, let me speak for once. I see you now as you are, as I saw you at first. You cannot sin as I can. You have lasting peace and there is no disorder in you, while within me all is violence. I have never really spoken to you about myself, I have never really spoken to you about anything, but this evening you must listen to me."

He broke off and looked straight into David's eyes, then went on speaking in a voice which roughened slightly.

"I wanted to be a saint, like the saints of old. From my childhood I was familiar with the idea that I would be the friend of God. I loved God. I loved God before fearing Him. Now it's all changed. I could not tell you what goes on inside me. I can't speak well enough for that. Words are my enemies and betray me. The hope that is in your heart is in mine too, but with it is a terrible fear. You have found God and He will never be taken away from you, but as for me, I tremble all the time that I may lose Him, because it seems that I am plunged deep in sin. I am on fire, David. If I do not sin with a woman it is because God preserves me as he preserved the Philistine Abimelech, but I have a dreadful desire for this sin which I do not commit. You don't know what this hunger of the body is like. I sometimes feel that I am separated from my flesh, and it is as though there were two people in me, one who suffered and the other who watched the sufferer."

Again he was silent. David bowed his head.

"You are right to speak to me," he said in a hesitating voice. "I think I should pray. I shall pray."

"There is a woman I think about," said Joseph rapidly.

Once more fear entered David's eyes.

"You mustn't," he whispered. "I don't want to know. It's not my business."

"But you know who it is. I want to tell you her name. I feel it would free me to say her name."

"I don't want you to tell me."

Joseph looked at him in silence.

"She comes between God and me," he said at last. "I hate her. At heart I hate her."

"You should not hate anyone."

They were silent, looking away from each other. After a moment Joseph rose.

"Probably I shouldn't have told you all I did," he said in a calmer voice, "but it was too much for me. For months I say nothing and then there comes a day when I can't bear any more. I think you are right when you say one should not hate anyone. You are always right. One way and another I am always wrong."

Without replying David picked up the pen he had put down and wrote a few words on the fly-leaf of the Shakespeare.

"If our heart condemn us . . ." Joseph read.

He nodded and slipped the little book in his pocket.

XVIII

THAT night he was again unable to sleep. His whole
conversation with David kept on coming back to him
and he mentally made the alterations he wanted, for the
recollection of several sentences which had escaped him
made him blush. Once again he had said just the things
he did not want to say. The words which came from his
lips in spite of himself always surprised him, because
they were a clear expression of things that until then had
been hidden deep inside him. For example, it was true
that formerly he had wanted to be a saint, but he had
never put this into words, never admitted it; he scarcely
knew that in the dark regions of his soul such thoughts
obsessed him. And suddenly he said that. Oh, if only
he could take back his words as one tears up a paper on
which one has written something foolish!

It was the same with what he had said about Moira.
But he must try not to think about Moira. He turned
from side to side in his bed, his eyes wide open. The
parlour clock struck three in a busy, impatient way;
then, far off in the night, the University clock spoke in
its turn, lazily, as if asleep.

He had never heard three o'clock in the morning strike
before. His hand groped for his little bedside lamp and
pressed the switch. The room became visible, but it
seemed to have been awakened from sleep, for everything had an unusual, almost frightening, appearance.
Propped on his right elbow, his chin in his palm, he
looked anxiously around him with large, sombre eyes.
The thoughts one has in the dark are not the same as
one has in the light. He knew that on turning off

the light he would once more become Moira's prey.

"She's not very beautiful." Twenty times a day he repeated that phrase to himself, for he knew he was right on that point, but what good was it to be right if she attracted him just the same? And she was dreadfully attractive. At the very instant when, his heart swelling with rage, he had stooped before her to pick up his sweater, he had lost his freedom. But it was only now that he realised it; at a few minutes past three on a cold November morning the suspicion came to him that he was lost, like the others.

His arm grew numb, but he did not move. Although nothing around him had altered, he had the impression that the objects were watching him, as in fairy-tales. Suddenly he threw back the blanket and got up. Since he could not sleep he would read.

He felt the icy air from the garden on his bare legs and went shivering to close the window. He instinctively picked up his Bible from the table, but put it down again at once. Would he not find in the pages of this book his own condemnation in black and white, as though he alone were meant? The texts were there in abundance.

He noticed that his teeth were chattering and looked around for a few seconds, then had the idea of glancing at the Shakespeare David had given him. Crossing the room, he felt in his coat pocket for the little book, and went back to bed, slipping with a shiver between the bedclothes, where he found the delicious warmth he had left.

For a moment he could do no more than hold the book open at eye level. Curled up with his legs twined round each other, he still trembled with cold, but gradually he became warmer. He flicked over several pages and came across the summary of *Othello*. He read it several times, idly at first, then with attention, trying to discover the meaning of the story, whose end in particular struck him as absurd and revolting. How was it possible for a man to kill the woman he loved? One only killed one's enemies. True, it was in a book; the story was invented, a lie. And then that negro smothering a white woman with a pillow . . . He could not understand why David thought it necessary to read such things. Was that knowledge of the human heart? Evidently the style mattered. Everyone knew that it was essential to have read Shakespeare.

What he himself suffered was not to be found in books, he did not recognise it even in poetry. And yet the single word, love, moved him strangely. To love God, to love one's neighbour, were expressions which for him kept their glowing freshness, but love was tenderness and joy, it could not be death, crime, terrible deeds. Why did there have to be sin in human love?

Turning back the pages, he came to the fly-leaf with the few words David had written and he looked at them until they became blurred, and the letters wavered before his eyes: "If our heart condemn us God is greater than our heart." He gently lifted the book to his face and pressed his lips to the words of the Beloved Disciple. A sudden feeling of affection bore him up. His joy in this minute was as great as his former anxiety and all the passion of which he was capable went into the kiss. It was as though his soul and his flesh, reconciled at last, had met at the exact place where his lips rested.

Without his even realising it, the book slid from his fingers and he fell asleep.

XIX

THE next day, after the last class of the morning, he went with David to the cafeteria. It was a long building, which might have been taken in the distance for a neo-Greek temple, and which seemed to be ashamed of its tall brick chimney, for it was hidden in a fold of ground behind the gymnasium. The two entered by a little side door and found themselves in a vast kitchen, where several women in white aprons were working. One of them came forward and jerked her head bad-temperedly. She was short and fat, with a shiny face, and putting one hand on her hip she let her disapproving stare mount from Joseph's feet to his face while he stood without moving. David underwent the same examination and nudged his friend to make him speak, but Joseph was silent.

"I don't want two men," said the woman.

David explained that he had come merely to introduce his friend.

"Yes, to introduce me," Joseph said with a gesture.

And he blushed.

"You understand you'll only work here at noon, not in the evening."

The two young men nodded.

"Go over there and get what you want," she ordered Joseph, indicating the other end of the kitchen.

David pressed Joseph's arm lightly and went away.

A quarter of an hour later Joseph went into the big dining-room of the restaurant. There were two long rows of marble-topped tables and, right at the end, a counter with the food: meat and vegetables at one end and desserts at the other. As they came in the students were given a tin tray and their cutlery, then chose their dishes and paid the bill before sitting down. Joseph's task here was to clear away as the customers left, but he was not the only person doing this. Five other boys waited, like him, against the walls, their hands behind their backs, each wearing a long white apron down to the ankles and a little drill jacket with metal buttons. With an affectation of ease they smiled at each other, or exchanged jokes, but Joseph was obviously unhappy in his new surroundings and looked straight in front of him at a spot on the opposite wall. His white apron was tight at the waist and he did not like the cut of the white jacket, which left the small of his back uncovered; besides, he felt as if people were laughing at him, and through the noise of conversation and the clatter of knives and forks he thought several times that he heard his own name mentioned. Perhaps someone was calling to him. In any case he preferred to pretend he had not heard. Probably some of the students he knew were in the room, but this thought merely increased his discomfort. Their looks seemed to touch him like hands on his body, on his face, his ears and, above all, on his hair. How often had he tried to flatten his hair, whose natural waves copied the movement of flames, just as its colour copied their vividness! He, who always wanted to pass unnoticed, could no more hide himself than a lighted torch can hide in a dark corner. And this apron, flapping

184

round his legs, looking like a skirt. . . . Perhaps that was why they were laughing.

Someone touched his shoulder.

"David!" he said, starting. "I didn't expect you."

"I came to see if everything was going all right," said David with a smile. "I'm only staying a minute."

"Everything's all right," Joseph said.

There was a kind of enthusiasm in his voice and eyes, and he added: "Especially when you're there! I mean there's a sort of comfort in your presence. Perhaps I shouldn't tell you that here. It's not the right place."

"Not at all. It's perfectly all right. But you shouldn't rely on anyone, not on me or on anyone else. Why do you look so upset?"

"Everyone's looking at me. It embarrasses me."

David shrugged his shoulders.

"Nobody's paying any attention to you. Watch the tables. I can see several boys who are already eating their dessert."

"Tell me if Killigrew's here."

"I don't see him" David said, glancing round the room. "Oh yes, there at the end. He's at the last table, near the counter."

"I don't like his being there."

"How odd you are! You only have to look the other way if you see him coming."

"And MacAllister?"

"I don't know. Anyway, look at yourself. What's the matter with you?"

"I can't get used to the noise," Joseph murmured.

His anxious eyes turned to David, who was preparing to leave.

"Stay here!" he said.

"I can't. We'll meet again this afternoon."

Joseph watched him go with a certain irritation, and he thought him rather hard, in spite of the parson's smile which was continually on his lips. He went so far as to regret his affectionate words, but once more he realised that he controlled his heart very badly. Perhaps David despised him for being so timid, for not daring even to look round and see if Killigrew and MacAllister were there. Still, he thought himself lucky not to have asked the question which burnt his tongue, for the person he really wanted to see—or not to see (he did not know which)—was Moira. She threw him into such confusion that he had nearly asked David if poor Simon was in the room, and the memory of that strange boy seemed a bad omen, for he tried not to think of him as he tried, for different reasons, not to think of Moira. The world was full of things and people he ought not to think of.

At that moment two or three boys got up and he went forward to clear away. He piled the dirty plates on a tray, not too clumsily, picked up the glasses, knives and forks, keeping his eyes lowered in case he caught anyone's eye, but under his drill jacket his heart was thumping. In his haste to finish he nearly let the crockery slide off the tray, which was tilted to the right, and although he avoided this accident the sweat poured off his forehead.

In the kitchen he was jostled. Did he think he was in a parlour? The plates there. Knives, forks and spoons in a pile in the sink. And back to the restaurant, quickly!

"Go on, get a move on!" cried the woman he had met first.

He vanished. In the restaurant nearly everyone was getting up and the boys in aprons picked up the crockery with a rapidity that Joseph tried in vain to imitate as they threw the tin utensils noisily on the trays. All this movement confused him, and although he tried to copy his companions' gestures his dazed air made him a butt for their sarcasm. One of them made him blush to the ears by asking if he was so slow because he was thinking of his girl-friend, but what most disconcerted Joseph was the way these men introduced oaths into ordinary conversation. The name of Christ was incessantly blasphemed, and each time Joseph received a shock and could not get accustomed to it. He wondered how they dared. . . . In his little home town no one swore like that, at least not unless they were drunk.

As he made his way to the kitchen with a dangerously poised tray he felt someone undo his apron strings and he looked desperately over his shoulder, but there were too many people near him for him to see who was responsible. But an imperious voice was raised.

"Leave him alone!" it ordered.

At the same time an energetic hand seized and re-tied the strings and Joseph saw Praileau retreating into the crowd. The voice he had just heard was his enemy's, whose proud head seemed to dominate all the others, and in spite of himself Joseph followed him with his eyes for several seconds.

In the kitchen he noticed that his hands were shaking and he suddenly felt tired, but he was sent back to the restaurant to finish clearing away, and once more through the clatter of crockery the name of Christ was insulted. He wondered what he ought to do. Very often at the

University, in fact almost every day, he had heard the holiest name in the world taken in vain, but it had never before given him this direct shock, which made him wince. His former concerns suddenly seemed ridiculous, or at least trivial, almost unreal. The only reality was the name which even in a blasphemy was uttered only by divine permission. The other reality, the reality of the flesh, the reality of desire, cruel as it sometimes was, seemed at that moment illusory. There were two kingdoms: that of God and that of the world and these two kingdoms were mutually exclusive in man's heart; without knowing it these boys who blasphemed the name of Christ were restoring an invisible order.

He was motionless, still holding a pile of plates.

"Well, brother, have you made up your mind?"

The speaker had black, gay eyes and round cheeks like a child. He went on: "Are you going to take those plates away, or are you getting ready for a circus act?"

Joseph swallowed, then in a voice hoarse with emotion said: "I would like to know if you who constantly have Christ's name on your lips . . ."

"What?" said the man, stretching over the table to pick up two glasses between his fingers.

". . . have ever found Him?"

"If I've ever found what, Rusty?"

"Jesus."

The man put down the glasses and turned to Joseph. "Is it your first year here?"

Joseph was silent. Once more he wondered why some words came to his lips and not others, but he could not help it; at such moments something broke the barriers of caution and fear.

"Listen, brother, no one's even sure that your Christ ever existed," went on the black-eyed man, throwing a handful of forks on to his tray.

"I'm sure."

He lowered his eyes, then forced himself to raise them, and the glance he gave the speaker was that of a visionary.

"I'm sure," he repeated firmly. "He is here, near us, near you."

These words were spoken with such conviction that the man threw an involuntary glance over his shoulder.

"O.K." he said, annoyed, "one of these days you can get up on a chair and tell us all about hell. In the meantime pick up your plates."

Joseph obeyed, red-faced. From the human point of view his words were probably ill-timed, but God, who saw him in secret, would no doubt judge differently. His heart swelled at this thought and, picking up his tray, he went back to the kitchen, where he was given a basin of hot water and several piles of crockery to wash.

XX

To stand on a chair and speak to the students about hell, about their souls, about sin; to save them from the undying flames, that was his vocation, and God had told him through the mouth of this stranger. Joseph felt the tears come to his eyes at the thought that he was chosen by Heaven. He was saved. Something inside him had been repeating it unceasingly for the last hour, and his heart was bursting with love, an immense, confused love, which embraced Christ and all his creatures. So it had

189

been necessary for him to enter this large room and to work there at clearing the tables, so that he might meet the unbeliever who would show him the way. But before that there had been David's advice to him to offer his services in the cafeteria. Further back still, there was the affair of the new suit, without which there would have been no question of Joseph's becoming a waiter. How far away it all seemed, but how closely everything was linked. God guided everything. One had only to put oneself in His hands.

He wanted to run and shout, but he was afraid of being laughed at. In the long avenue, swept by the icy wind, he began to walk more quickly, his hands in the pockets of his overcoat. The sky might be grey and the trees bare, and the cold might reign over the whole earth and even over men's hearts, but he was filled with a joy no one could ever take away from him. He remembered his temptations, but distantly, as though they were someone else's temptations. This spiritual exaltation was so strong that he went past Mrs. Ferguson's house without seeing it and had to come back when he had reached the first houses of the town.

He went into David's room without knocking. David was sitting at his table and looked at him questioningly.

"I've got to talk to you," Joseph said, looking at the wall. "Yes, something has happened."

"At the cafeteria?" said David, anxiously. "Don't walk up and down like that. Take off your overcoat and sit down."

Joseph did not appear to hear him. After a moment he stood still and said: "I am called, David. As you are. Called by Christ. I feel it. I know it."

"But I've known it for a long time," David said, leaving his chair. "We've spoken about it. It's nothing new."

Joseph stood in the middle of the room.

"I did not know it as I know it today. Just now, among all those boys who were blaspheming, Christ's name sounded in me like a clap of thunder. I . . ."

He did not finish his sentence. David approached him.

"You don't have to tell me to make me understand," he said in a low voice. "I've always been sure that God had chosen you."

They were so close that their shoulders touched as they silently looked out at the trees in the little garden.

"Do you remember the night we prayed together?" David asked at last. "That night it seemed to me that He was near us."

"I know," Joseph said. "It seemed . . ."

"Do you think He would love us both so much if we were damned?"

Joseph did not answer this question, but his hand seized David's and pressed it lightly. Several minutes went by and neither felt like speaking. Suddenly David broke the silence by murmuring: "Look, its snowing."

Flakes were falling slowly in the grey light between the black branches, which were hardly visible. A shiver ran over Joseph and he was about to say that he did not like the snow, but it was not quite true; snow was the joy of childhood. And yet the whiteness weaving in the twilight made him uneasy. He felt that a curtain was falling before the approaching night to hide it from his eyes, and his heart ached.

David lit the lamp and let down the blind. How pleasant it now seemed between these four walls! On the ceiling the yellow circle shone softly and the rows of books absorbed a little of the peaceful light. The two young men sat facing each other, and Joseph recounted what had happened at the cafeteria, how, through the noise and blasphemies, he had thought he heard the voice from among all those voices, and how at once he seemed to become another man. It was like a miracle.

"But it is a miracle," David observed. "The greatest miracles are like that. The resurrection of Lazarus is not more astonishing than the return of the soul to God."

"I wish I could speak like you!" Joseph cried.

And, moved by an irresistible impulse, he confided his desire to address a crowd, to wrest people from the Devil. In his home town he had seen men suddenly get up and announce God's message with an amazing power of persuasion. Once a little carpenter, who was never seen at church, got on a soap box and spoke like a man possessed by the spirit of prophecy mentioned in Corinthians; three women had been converted then and there; everyone cried Hallelujah!

David expressed suspicion of these spontaneous preachers.

"One must be quite sure what one is doing," he said.

"One must give oneself up to the Spirit when the Spirit takes hold of you!" Joseph exclaimed, with shining eyes. "Here in this city of the plain that is our University thousands of souls are in peril of eternal fire. God wishes them to be warned. If necessary I myself will speak to them. I will get up on a chair and tell them about hell."

"But you've often told me you don't know how to speak."

"I shall know, if I have to."

"What, in fact, do you intend to do?"

"Get the students together, anywhere, in my room or in the open air, yes, and rouse them, David, rouse them until the fear of God makes them crawl like sick beasts, do you hear? I have the fear of God in me, and I shall force it into their very bones, until their bowels are melted, as the Scripture has it, and they cannot so much as look a woman in the face. Most of them incur damnation almost without knowing it, because they have no religion and they rush to hell like beasts. They're like beasts when they go to the prostitutes in the town. . . ."

David's calm voice interrupted him.

"Joseph, it needs a great deal of courage to get up on a chair and face scoffers."

Something seemed to pass over Joseph's face and his features altered suddenly.

"God will give the courage," he said. "Everything comes from God. You are not one of the scornful, you have never sat in that seat mentioned in the first Psalm, but you do not yet believe in me. Your love for God is peaceful, but I am mad for God. I can only love violently, because I am a passionate man. That is why I am more in danger of losing grace and why, in a way, I am nearer hell than you will ever be. You don't know what hell is, but I know, because I know what fire is. Fire is my home. Once, as a child, I was thrown into the blaze of God's presence; I can understand the burning in the hearts of the Apostles at Emmaus and the burning in Wesley's heart on the night of May 24. But there is also the blaze lit by the absence of God. For God is fire, David, and so much so that the horror of his non-presence is also expressed by fire, by black fire . . ."

"What are you saying?" David asked. "You talk as though you had visions."

"I'm speaking of what exists," Joseph went on, trying to soften his hoarse voice. "Since childhood I have done almost nothing but think of heaven and hell, and I know that the elect burn with love, as the damned burn with anger and hate. When I read the Bible I sometimes feel that my heart is on fire. That consoles me more than anything. We shall burn, David, we shall burn in an eternity of joy."

Now he was speaking in such a low voice that the sound of his words hardly disturbed the silence.

"We are separated from heaven only by the thickness of a flame. After this life . . . That must be said. People do not understand."

David looked at him without answering.

"Listen," said Joseph, after a hesitation, "I want to confess something. You must not interrupt me. You must not stop me speaking. I want you to know, even if you think it ridiculous."

"What is it?"

"The suit I'm wearing during the week, when it was meant to be kept for Sundays. . . ."

"Yes."

"Well, I put it on to please a woman. I was hoping to see her in the library, or even at church, although I don't suppose she goes to church very often. You know the woman I mean. I wanted her, David. I had already sinned with her in my heart when I saw her that day

I went to her room to get my sweater."

"You mustn't think of that any more."

"I don't think of it now. It's finished. But I had to tell you."

They were silent, both equally embarrassed by this confession. After a few more moments Joseph went away.

XXI

AFTER dinner that evening he left David earlier than usual and went to his room as nine o'clock was striking. Going towards the window to let down the blind, he watched the snow falling incessantly into the little garden along the side of the road. By the light of the street-lamps he could see the trees, whose branches were already bending and curving, crested with snow; they formed a criss-cross pattern against the dark background of the sky, a strangely delicate design, which caught the attention like a mysteriously complicated monogram. Joseph leant his forehead against the window-pane in order to see better when he heard behind him the slight noise of a key in the lock and, turning round, he saw Moira.

She was standing a few paces away from him, calmly slipping her fingers into the top of her dress.

"Yes, it's me," she said.

The young man did not move. The woman seemed to be wavering backwards and forwards in a kind of mist.

"Don't look at me as though I were the Devil," she went on.

Her voice was low, with singing inflexions. She began to smile at Joseph's silence.

"Why don't you say something?" she asked.

He noticed that she was wearing a black dress, which left her arms bare above the elbows, and in the uncertain light of the little bedside lamp she had a dignity he had never seen in her before. For a moment or two he even wondered if she were the same arrogant, hard young woman he remembered; her voice in particular seemed different, almost caressing in its tenderness, in spite of a certain irony of intonation. And yet he recognised the over-red mouth, which he glanced at furtively.

She looked round the room.

"Boys' rooms are queer," she said. "Nothing's left about. . . ."

"Go away!" he said suddenly.

"Oh no, Mr. Day! I've been waiting for you for more than a quarter of an hour. Look, I've spread my coat out on your bed to dry."

He followed her pointing finger and saw the navy-blue coat on the bedspread. Without moving he repeated in a low voice: "Go away!"

"No, I'm not going. In any case if you wanted to make me go you'd have to get your key from where I've put it" (she placed her hand on her breast) "and I hope you wouldn't dare."

The last words were spoken with a little laugh—the sly laugh of a schoolgirl, and she added: "It gives me a queer feeling having the key against my skin. It's burning and freezing at the same time. A bit like you, by the way, from all one hears."

He blushed.

"Why have you come here?" he asked.

"I'll tell you later. I've decided to spend a certain number of hours here. Mind you, if my presence gives you what are commonly called ideas I advise you to get rid of them at once. That's not what I've come for, believe me."

He felt his anger rise, and took a step towards Moira, who did not move.

"May I sit down?" she asked gently.

He was taken aback by this question and stood still. She walked straight towards him and, without looking at him, went and sat down a yard away in the arm-chair.

"Very well," he said, with an effort at self-control, "if you won't leave this room, I shall."

"What about the key?" she asked, rocking herself. "How will you open the door without the key?"

He pointed to the window.

"Oh, no," she said with a smile. "If you so much as touch that window I shall scream so loudly that people will think someone's being murdered. I can make a lot of noise when I like. And what a scandal that would be, Mr. Day! They'd find a woman in your room . . ."

"It would be as harmful to you as to me."

"Not at all. It's all the same to me. But not to you, is it?"

He looked at her with wild eyes. His mind had been so confused during the last few minutes that he could not think what to say. He could not force this woman to leave his room, because of the appalling scandal which would result. It seemed equally impossible to talk to her, to persuade her. She had an answer for everything, and in any case he was no good at talking. In a flash he saw himself on his knees, begging her to go away; the mere thought of such a humiliating attitude increased his anger. Moira would laugh at him. Her gentle, almost modest appearance had surprised him for a moment, but this imitation of a young lady visiting was all a pretence, though she did almost look like someone calling on a neighbour and trying to think what to say. Above all, Joseph dreaded the laugh he had just heard and his blood sang in his ears with rage.

Suddenly he remembered what Killigrew had told him: they wanted to play a trick on him. That was it. His ideas about religion and morality were well known; they would think it amusing to get a woman into his room, and Moira would readily lend herself to the practical joke. What a relief! If the whole thing were only a trick it was not so bad.

"How long are you going to stay?" he asked.

She leant her head against the back of the chair, and her large, sea-green eyes were dreamy.

"For hours," she said. "I told you."

He lowered his head and noticed that she was wearing little rubber boots up to her calves to protect her legs from the snow and, although he could not explain it to himself, they struck him as cruel and improper. He looked away.

"Does that annoy you?" she asked.

"What?"

"My staying."

"Oh, no," he said with a shrug.

He laughed.

"You laugh very badly," Moira said. "You don't really feel like laughing and you hate me."

"I wish you'd go away!" he burst out.

"Don't keep on repeating that or I shall get obstinate and then . . . And besides, you should never let anyone know what you're trying to get from them. Didn't you know that?"

She rocked herself insolently and for a few moments there was no sound except the creaking of the chair on the floor. From where he stood Joseph was almost directly in front of Moira, whose face was lit in such a way that half of it was in the shadow. She was smaller than he had thought, and more fragile. Her black hair and shining eyes, and something delicate about her whole person, made one think of a bird. Suddenly the scent she was covered in reached his nostrils, a faint odour of lilac, so fine that it was at once dissipated; he recognised it and experienced a curious emotion, partly of pleasure and partly of irritation caused by that pleasure.

"Why don't you look straight at me?" she asked. "You look like a guilty child."

He said nothing. She went on rocking and then asked: "Are you scared, Mr. Day?"

"Scared? Scared of whom?"

"Why, of yourself."

It was like a slap in the face and he felt himself redden. She added very low, like someone speaking in the dark: "Not of me, I'm sure."

"I'm not scared of anyone," he said, with a gesture.

Again she uttered her sly laugh, which wounded him more than the harshest words. Apparently she was amused by him, by his awkward ways, but she seemed to notice the effect her mockery had on Joseph, and was abruptly silent.

"Could you give me a drink?" she asked at last, with affected shyness.

Without answering, he took his water-bottle off the mantelpiece and filled a glass, which he handed to Moira. She looked at him open-mouthed.

"Water!" she said, astonished.

He stood before her, holding the glass of water.

"Mr. Day," Moira said, "your innocence is . . ."

She tried in vain to find the right word and finally said: ". . . horrible!"

He looked straight at her.

"Where do you come from?" she asked.

He mentioned his home town.

"Ah," she said as though that explained the glass of water and everything else, "from the hills . . ."

"Yes, from the hills," he said, without moving.

"Here," she said in a harsh, almost masculine voice, "when we talk about drinking we mean alcohol."

"Alcohol. . . ."

Moira saw a flash of anger in Joseph's eyes and his hand trembled. Realising his intention, she suddenly hit out at the hand which held the glass. The water spilled on the floor between them. With a push of her heel the young woman began rocking again.

"I'm sorry," she said, "but you were just going to do something silly." (She laughed softly.) "You were going to chuck that water in my face."

He put the glass back on the mantelpiece.

"You must admit you have a shocking disposition," she said, looking at him, "and you don't know how to talk to a woman."

"I don't want to talk to you," he said, folding his arms.

"Do you think I hadn't gathered that? That's what amuses me."

Without pursuing this, he crossed the room and sat down on the edge of the bed, near the little table, where the lamp was shining. With an automatic gesture he picked up his Bible, but put it down again at once, as though it were impossible to read the Scriptures in the presence of this woman. In reality he was ashamed and afraid of being laughed at. Instead of the Bible he opened the little Shakespeare David had given him.

Moira went on rocking for a few minutes, then got up and made a tour of the room. Her rubbers muffled the sound of her footsteps and she walked about the room as though she had been alone, looking at the old-fashioned engravings on the walls. Not once did she look at the young man, but out of the corner of her eye she noticed his studious attitude as he bent over his book, his legs crossed and his pugnacious profile silhouetted against the lampshade. His hair gilded by the light fell like a sheaf over his low forehead and his jet-black eyes glittered under his eyebrows. She passed quite near him in order to examine a sampler in a black frame, which was hung near the bed. It consisted of the alphabet and above it in Gothic letters: "God bless our home!" At last, having satisfied her curiosity, she went back to the middle of the room and said suddenly: "Mr. Day, I have a letter to write. Will you let me have some paper."

He raised his head.

"You'll find everything you want there, in the drawer of my table," he said calmly.

She sat down at the table, which stood against the wall about a yard from the bed.

"But I can't see here," she said.

He silently moved the lamp so that its rays fell on the young woman's hands. After a short hesitation Moira took a sheet of paper and an envelope out of the drawer, and began to write.

"My dear Selina, So far, nothing. Generally when I'm alone with a man something happens, but today's customer is a bit different from the others. You can laugh if you like: I'm not laughing. I'm bored and I wish the whole thing was over. To be frank, I don't much like the way things are going.

"I got into his room without difficulty. I don't have to tell you that here you can walk into people's houses without any difficulty. Knowing I had to deal with rather a queer bird, I locked the door and put the key in the top of my dress. I knew, of course, that if he started poking about there he was lost, but he seems to realise it too. In any case, he's furious with me. Usually that's a good sign, for anger, my child, is a form of desire and nothing is nearer caresses than blows. What spoils the present situation is that he has decided to sulk. He's reading, or pretending to."

Without moving her head, she raised her eyes and risked a glance at Joseph.

"You can't imagine how vicious he looks when he's reading," she went on. "You could swear he was going to bite. And he's even redder than I thought. I don't like red-heads. Their skins are milky and this one is so smooth. Sometimes he looks like a very beautiful woman. Yes, he's like the Republic, or Liberty giving light to the world. He's not my type. Perhaps you think I find it funny, but on consideration I don't want to make fun of him at all. I wish he would make advances, very nicely, so that I could send him about his business and get out of here. I madly want to smoke, but I left my case in MacAllister's room and, as you can well imagine, the Exterminating Angel doesn't smoke. I asked him just now for a drink, and he gave me a glass of water. The Biblical cup of cold water. I knew he was crazy, but even so it took my breath away. If ever he fell in love with a woman he would be very boring. He would respect her, which would be worse than anything.

"I'm going on writing, although I shall see you in a couple of hours, because I must do something, but I'll post this letter as I go out: we'll have a good laugh tomorrow afternoon. Actually I can't go away without appearing ridiculous in the eyes of this gentleman, who would be sure to think he had got the better of me. I thought at one point that he was going to hit me. One can always come to an understanding with a man who hits you; it starts a discussion which may become interesting, but he controlled himself just in time. I must confess that he had the idea of throwing his Biblical cup of cold water in my face, but I stopped him because of the damage it would have done to my perm, my powder, etc. I'd have looked like a drowned rat. Mind you, I don't despair of seeing him on his knees before me. I know men and what they're thinking about, but it's going to be a long business and it's already half-past nine. At the moment he seems not to be paying me any attention, but the idiot is forgetting to turn over the pages. I shouldn't be surprised if he was holding the book upside down, like the young man in the park James told us about.

"It's very difficult to seduce a fool. I'm rather sorry

I tried. You'd think a few well-chosen insults would be enough to put fire into their veins and set them flaming like a Christmas pudding, but this man is in a class of his own. His immobility is rather frightening. I'd like to shout 'Joseph!' and make him jump as he sits there bending over his book. He doesn't imagine the trouble he's giving me. He's like an actor who doesn't know his cue. The play's brought to a standstill. I can't stay here all night just writing what comes into my head. I'd end up by telling you what I really thought! When he bent down in my room to pick up his sweater I noticed what a good figure he had. Don't go drawing conclusions; I only put that in to fill up space. Anyway I've nothing more to say. You egged me on to take on MacAllister's stupid dare. You thought I was so sure of myself, so arrogant, didn't you? Let's say it. And whenever a good-looking boy turns up he's always for Moira first, isn't he? You thought that perhaps it wouldn't work with the Exterminating Angel. You don't really like me at heart, Selina, you're simply scared of me. But I'm not the floosie you all think. I'm tired of just being an instrument of pleasure."

She carefully crossed out the last six lines, so that they were illegible, and added: "I've lost, Selina. I'm the one who's in love."

For the last quarter of an hour Joseph had been sitting perfectly still and his right hand was beginning to go to sleep, but it was as though he thought that by not moving he could keep the danger in check. Ten or twelve times already he had read and re-read, without understanding it, Othello's speech before the Doge and Senators of Venice:

"Most potent, grave and reverend signiors . . ."

Perhaps David would be inspired to knock at his door. What would he do then? A few hours before they had both been talking about Heaven. And now . . . this! But he would explain everything to David. How he wished he had told him what Killigrew had said about the trick that was going to be played on him! The woman was still writing. How long would she stay? She wrote very slowly, stopping on purpose, but the moment would come when she had had enough, and then she would go away. Over the top of his book he saw her head and part of her bosom. She showed her bosom as she bent over; the position of her body did that: her bust was compressed and so it bulged. Perhaps she did not realise he could see, but Killigrew had implied that she was just the same as a loose woman and women like that exposed themselves, exposed parts of their bodies, their arms, their bosom. There was one in his home town, but it was wrong to look at her, only the lost souls dared. It was known that the boy at the drug store had given her three dollars to commit evil with her; there were others too, who did not admit it. She was called Goldie, because of her hair, and she, too, showed her bosom, but he had never thought about her; when he saw her in the distance he simply crossed the street and she did not exist for him, and if he was thinking of her now it was because of Moira; yet Moira was more beautiful, in spite of the red on her mouth. Her eyes were very large. Her skin shone like satin on her shoulders and throat. She was there, so close to him that he could hear her breathing. She had come to play a trick on him. Luckily he had known. "If you have what are called ideas"—no, it was: "what are commonly called ideas . . ." He did not quite know what she meant. Perhaps kissing her on the mouth, or even doing evil with her. Doing evil with her. But she would go away when she saw that he was resolved not to move. Doing with her what the boy from the drug store did with Goldie. That was why she had said: "If you have what are commonly called ideas . . ." Perhaps she hoped he would go down on one knee and declare his love, as in a play, and then she could laugh in his face. But he would not move. He would stay there like a statue until she got tired of seeing him like that. Then she would go away. She would take the key from where she had put it, in the opening of her dress, between her two breasts. She would open the door and go away and she could not say he had made a declaration, she could not laugh at him, she would not dare.

Little by little he felt calmer and stronger. It was not his fault if he wanted her. His man's body wanted her, but the body led one to hell if one gave way to it. What his body wanted his soul did not want. Like St. Paul he had a thorn in his flesh, a messenger of Satan to buffet him. Because of this the blood was beating in his temples and his entrails were taut. And there was something else as well, something painful and humiliating which he could not help.

Why was the woman writing so quickly? Now she was crossing out what she had written and writing something else. Now she was taking an envelope and writing the address and sealing the envelope.

"Mr. Day, would you give me a stamp?" she said in a low voice.

A slight impulse of avarice made him hesitate, then he said without raising his eyes: "There's a little cardboard box in the drawer and you'll find a book of stamps there."

"Thank you."

He heard her searching for the stamp in the drawer and, with his eyes fixed on the page of the little book, wondered what she would do next. Write another letter? He would not bear it. He would snatch the paper away. She had no right to be there and he wanted to beat her, but every time he let his eyes stray over the edge of his book his anger gave place to a great misgiving. Fragments of sentences he had heard when he was at Mrs. Dare's came into his mind, all the things the students said about women, such definite terms that he could not forget them.

She stuck the stamp on the envelope and said: "You'll be glad to hear that I'm going, Mr. Day."

He made such a sudden gesture that he dropped the book.

"You're going?" he said, astonished.

"Yes. Why the surprise?"

He felt himself redden, and bent down to pick up the little Shakespeare.

"I'm not surprised," he murmured, "only you said you would stay for hours."

"Well, I've changed my mind," she said, rising, the letter in her hand.

Again he noticed her rubbers and turned away his eyes. Straightening up, he kept his head down, for his cheeks and ears were still burning and he was ashamed of the flush which persisted against his will.

"Women are always changing their minds," she went on. "Didn't you know?"

He got up too and put the lamp in its usual place.

"Give me back my key, please," he said.

"I can open the door by myself," Moira replied, walking towards it. "Or perhaps you're afraid I'll keep your key," she added with a smile.

"Yes," he said as he followed her.

Her mouth opened in surprise.

"I don't think you quite know what you're saying, Mr. Day."

Joseph bit his lip; she was right. He did not quite know what he was saying. Suddenly he looked so crest-fallen that Moira began to laugh.

"You'll get your key back!"

She raised her hand to her breast.

"Oh, it's slipped!" she said in confusion. "Your key has slipped. I must . . . don't look, please."

He turned round violently to face the wall and folded his arms while she felt under her dress. After a moment he heard the key fall on the floor.

"You can turn round," Moira said.

He obeyed and looked straight into her eyes.

"What are you going to tell your friends?" he asked.

"Nothing. The truth."

"You're not going to tell them I made you a declaration?"

She burst out laughing.

"A declaration! You've shown me the door! Go on, pick up your key. Don't stand there withering me with your glance, Mr. Day. Pick up your key."

He bent down and seized the key, which was warm to

his touch. At the same instant he felt Moira's fingers deep in his hair.

"Savage!" she murmured, in an almost inaudible voice.

He leapt to his feet.

"Why did you touch me?" he cried.

She recoiled with her back to the door and her face went white. In the half-light she saw Joseph's eyes shining like the eyes of no other man she had ever seen, and she was suddenly filled with terror.

"Open the door!" she said.

He took a step towards her. She felt the young man's breath on her forehead and eyes as he stretched out his neck like an animal.

"No!" said Moira in a low voice. "No! I don't want to! I don't want to!"

XXII

HE was roused from his sleep by a feeling of being smothered, and with a sudden gesture he threw back the heavy blanket, which almost covered his mouth. His eyes went to the ceiling. He saw a light he did not at first recognise, which looked a little like the reflection of a fire, and he instinctively looked towards the fireplace, but it was not lit. Then he remembered that during the struggle the lamp had rolled under the bed without breaking.

His body was streaming with sweat; he raised one knee to push back the heavy blanket and in the faint light saw his own naked body. He automatically turned away his eyes. Against his side, nestled in his arm was that other body, whose contented breathing brushed his chest. Gradually each detail fell into place in his memory: the woman who struggled and pleaded with him, on the floor, where they had fallen, then on this bed, and that sudden consent, that incomprehensible surrender. She had yielded all at once; all at once she had become like a beast. . . . He placed his hand on that flesh, so terribly soft, and sprang up.

His teeth were chattering with cold and he felt a shudder run over him from his head to his feet. Killigrew's description came back to him: *lupa*, the wolf. That was Moira and that was love. He put on his dressing-gown, tying it furiously round his waist, then went back to the bed, where Moira, her eyes still closed, put out a sleepy hand towards the empty place.

"Wake up!" he ordered.

She passed the back of her hand over her face and half opened her eyes.

"I'm cold!" she murmured.

"You're cold," he said, in an altered voice.

And gathering up the large, grey blanket, which had slipped on to the floor, he suddenly let it fall on the girl's head. Moira's convulsive leap nearly threw her out of the bed, but Joseph kept her down with all his strength under the great mass of wool, from which a moan escaped, like the cry of a baby.

"You're cold!" he repeated with fury. "You're cold, Moira!"

The little body turned in all directions with an extraordinary violence. It was suddenly full of such energy that Joseph was afraid it would break free, and his hands plunged so deeply into the blanket that through all its thickness he could feel the shape underneath.

He panted as he bent over her. Disconnected words came from his lips, and at one moment he was crying, without noticing it. When she was quite still he gave a deep sigh and raised the blanket, but at the sight of that face looking at him he took a step backwards in silence.

He dressed her. To put on her frock he had to bend her arms, which were still warm, and with clumsy hands he tried to arrange her hair; he wanted above all to brush aside the dark locks which fell like a curtain down to her chin. Then he spread a clean handkerchief over the dead woman's face. It made her seem less terrifying. He put her shoes on her feet, together with the rubbers, but when he had picked up her stockings and underclothes from the floor, he rolled them together and held them for a moment, undecided what to do with them. Finally, he put them in the pocket of the navy-blue coat and wrapped Moira's body in it.

All this was done slowly and with care. His face wore a mask of stupor and his mouth was half-open. When he had finished he let himself fall on his back beside the dead woman and fell into a heavy sleep.

After a long time he dreamed that someone was shaking his shoulder to wake him, and he opened his eyes. The same firelight was on the ceiling. He closed his eyes so as not to see it, and tried to sleep again, but his memory took him over all the events of that night with pitiless clarity. He lay motionless for a few minutes, then felt for his watch in the drawer of his bedside table. It was a quarter past two.

The thing he did not want to see was by his side, almost touching him, in that dark blue coat with a handkerchief over its face. In a low voice, as though he were afraid of waking someone, he said slowly: "A quarter past two."

Suddenly he got up and put on his clothes, the dark-grey suit he had worn to please a woman; and the woman was there, in his bed. Nothing he was doing seemed real. But he had made up his mind. After he had put on his trousers and jacket he had to bend down and lace his shoes, then come back to the bed and lift Moira under the arms and legs, carry her away. She could not stay there.

He picked her up like a child. She was light, in spite of the heavy coat and the boots, but suddenly he remembered that the door was locked and he had to lay his burden back on the bed, find the key in his trouser pocket and open the door.

Now he was silently going along the passage to the back door, and he passed David's room. There was not the slightest sound in the whole house, except his own breathing in the dark. Moira's arms hung over Joseph's right shoulder and he held her round the waist, pressed her close. In his bedroom the handkerchief had fallen off. Joseph had not been able to help seeing her face, now quite dark.

When he reached the door he turned the key too quickly in the lock and there was a click which seemed to fill the night with the sound of a shot. He waited a moment, then opened the door and went down the steps. The cold whipped his face. It was still snowing, but although the sky was so dark a kind of diffused light from the ground made it possible to see a little. Joseph knew that he had only to keep straight on, and for a few moments he floundered in the snow, his face caressed by the flakes, some of them catching in his eyelashes, others stinging his lips.

When he had reached the low wall he gently put Moira's body down on the snow and went into the shed, where he felt round the walls for the garden tools David had shown him. He took a spade and threw it over the wall, then bent down again and picked up the body. The wall was just low enough for him to step over. For a moment he wandered under the trees, then he was afraid of going too far and not being able to find the spade. Where he now was he could not be heard from the house. He must put the body down, go back and find the spade at the foot of the wall.

It took him some time to do all this, but now he was digging in the earth, as he used to when he worked in the fields; but tonight the earth was hardened by the cold and resisted the bite of the spade, and it was too dark for the young man to judge the depth of the grave without getting into it from time to time and feeling round the deep, black hole. The reflected light from the snow enabled him to make the grave an even shape and he forced himself to go on digging until his hands trembled with weariness. When at last, going down once more into the grave, he found it up to his chest, he stopped, exhausted. Above his head, between the branches, hundreds of flakes floated towards him. He thought: 'If it goes on snowing I'm saved.'

Taking the body under the shoulders and knees, he put it in the grave and covered the head with part of the coat. At this point he hesitated. Fragments of the office for the dead came into his head, the words of Job and of St. John, which the minister recites as he goes slowly to the altar, followed by the men bearing the coffin: "Man that is born of a woman is of few days . . . I am the Resurrection and the Life. He that believeth in me . . ." But he could not utter a sound. He climbed out of the hole and began to fill it with earth.

As he went back across the garden the snow was still falling, obliterating his footsteps, obliterating everything. Back in his room he took off his clothes and slipped naked into the icy bed. He could not stop shivering; at last he grew warmer and fell asleep.

XXIII

"And yet God has not said a word!"
ROBERT BROWNING

It was nearly seven when he woke and dressed in the usual way. It was still snowing. From the road came a sound of shovels scraping the pavement, but it was still dark, and although he pressed his face against the window, the white curtain falling from the sky to the earth hid everything.

Nothing was altered in the room. Only the disorder of the bed seemed unusual; Joseph took care to straighten the sheets and blankets and shake up the pillow, so as to give everything its normal appearance. The lamp was put back on the table and it was then that he noticed Moira's letter in its envelope. His first impulse was to open it, but a scruple stopped him. He had never yet read a letter which was not addressed to him. For a long time he held it in his hands, undecided, then slipped it into his pocket and looked round him, as though looking for something, even glancing under the furniture. But there was nothing, there remained nothing; everything was over there, in the hole under the snow.

Going back to the bed he turned down a corner of the sheet and bent over the pillow; the persistent scent was the only thing which made him anxious. It rose from the bed like a warm body, a scent of flesh mingled with the perfume of lilac, a living, rebellious scent. Joseph turned back the bedclothes and crossed the room to throw the window wide open. The icy air swept in like a flood. The young man turned off the light and shivered. Beyond the veil of snow, far over in the greying sky, the day was breaking. He watched, motionless and trembling with cold; he did not say his prayers.

Shortly afterwards he was having breakfast with David, alone with him just as usual, and David was talking to him in his gentle voice, offering him bread and coffee, and another was answering him and eating. That was what seemed stranger to Joseph than anything: he was there and another was acting in his place; in some way he himself was not there. He could not explain it. He had not the words, there were some things he could never explain.

He wondered if the perfume in his room had disappeared. David had not noticed anything; he had merely remarked: "You ought to close your window. Look at the snow on the floor." And Joseph had closed it; the other had closed it.

In the history class that morning he took advantage of

an empty place at the back of the hall and sat there safe from all curious glances, for he felt that people were looking at him even more than usual. No doubt it was, as always, because of his red hair, but today he could not bear it.

With folded arms and eyes fixed on a map of the United States pinned to the blackboard, he fell into a kind of numbness like a stupor. It was warm in the class, almost too warm. He wanted to go to sleep and the professor's voice was so monotonous that his words ran into each other, as though forming one word, and he could not understand him. Joseph wanted to shut his eyes, but did not dare. Outside it was no longer snowing. That was a remarkable thing. It was still snowing when Joseph came into the hall, but now it was not snowing, and in Joseph's mind the sentence repeated itself twice, ten times, twenty times, until he realised its full force: 'The snow has stopped.' It had fallen for hours and hours and now it was over; the sun shone in the icy blue sky.

For hours the snow . . . since four o'clock on the day before until a quarter past nine this morning. That was a long time. But since the night, since the middle of the night until now, was how long? Seven hours perhaps, perhaps more. For seven hours the snow, which now sparkled in the sun, had been falling. It would be cleared away in the streets, but elsewhere, in the woods, it would lie for days and days, until the end of the winter. And there would be more snow, all through the winter, and under that snow there were all the dead leaves, which the wind shifted, that thick layer of dead leaves smoothed out by the wind as by a great hand. Yet it was a fact that the snow was no longer falling and Joseph looked out of the window with wide-open eyes.

When the class was over he got up with the others and went out. He was jostled, for he stood without moving on the steps, dazzled by the sparkling blanket, which made him blink. A path had been dug in the snow, which was more than knee-deep, and it was the only way of reaching the covered arcades, but many of the students ran on to the lawn, whooping like Indians, and had mock fights, gathering handfuls of the soft, white stuff to smear the faces of their opponents. Someone called to Joseph, but he did not answer. He walked on with his hands in the pockets of his overcoat and did not notice that his history book had fallen from under his arm. That was perhaps why he was being called, but he did not hear. When he was in the East Lawn he walked more quickly to pass a group of students.

He went down a few steps, skirted the library and reached the great avenue. At that moment the orange street-car, which stopped a little further on, passed him and Joseph began to run and jumped on the platform. The people moved up to make room for him. The snow seemed to have put everyone in a good temper; it was the first snow of the year, still unblemished, and the traces of childhood that are in everyone's heart greeted the fairy-like disappearance of all colour. But in town the snow was already dirty; the roads were banked on either side and on the pavements the passers-by trampled in the mud.

Joseph got off at the railway station, which was the terminus. It was a dirty yellow building, discoloured black near the roof. He crossed the waiting-room and sat down on the long oak bench with its curved back and remained there for a few minutes without moving. Several people looked at him, staring at his hair, and he regretted having come out without a hat. A sailor asked him for a match, but instead of answering, Joseph got up awkwardly and went out. He preferred to leave rather than speak to a stranger.

There was a small café opposite the station and he went in for a cup of coffee, but once inside he came out again. There were too many people looking at him, as in the waiting-room. Ordinarily he did not mind, but today was different.

Without knowing why, he went up the main street. His feet seemed to move of their own accord, leading him where they would, as in a dream. It was strange not to know what to do with oneself, with one's body. But the body had to be somewhere, to breathe, to move.

A large store, painted red, caught his eye. A crowd of people were jostling at the glass doors, going in and out. He followed them, almost relieved to feel his will overwhelmed by the mass will of the crowd, and he let himself be carried along, like a straw in a torrent.

He came out. For some minutes now neuralgia seemed to be pressing an iron crown on his head and he wondered why he did not go back to the University. He wanted to lie down, not on his own bed, but on David's bed, in that warm, peaceful room, where nothing unpleasant could ever happen. David would talk to him in his reasonable tones, would not ask him questions. And Joseph would sleep. If only he could sleep everything would be all right. There were too many people in the streets, too many people everywhere, too many faces looking at him with silent interrogation.

Standing in the mud, he waited for the orange street-car. He noticed two little stores on the opposite side of the road, one almond green, the other red. The green one was a cleaner's, whose proprietor was called Ward, and the red one had a Chinese name over the door, followed by the word "Laundry". Something inside him was interested in these details, trying to imagine the lives of these unknown people, their faces, their mutual relations. Perhaps Ling-ho was happy, or perhaps Ward taunted him harshly because of his race and the colour of his skin, making fun of his comic English. Perhaps, too, the laundryman was not honest, for after all he was only a pagan, and he probably had a yellow wife, yellow as ivory, and children who spoke a language made up of little cries. . . .

The arrival of the street-car put an end to these imaginings; Joseph sat just behind the driver; in that way he could not see the people looking at him, for as he passed along they raised their eyes, as usual. At least three hundred people could say as they went home that morning: "I saw a red-haired man in the street, a red-haired man with a queer face." The sailor who had spoken to him would remember him, too. In the street-car he felt more sheltered than on the pavement, and he was reassured by the sound of the wheels on the rails, but each stop frightened him. He wished there were no stops and that the street-car would go on endlessly from street to street, then on the high road and into the country, for hours, until it reached the little town in the hills. At home the snow probably came to mid-thigh and from time to time a heavy white mass would slide off a roof with a rumble like thunder. In the old days Joseph could hear it from his bed. It was one of the things that always reminded him of his childhood, that and the strange light the snow threw on the ceiling of his little room.

He suddenly noticed that he had passed his stop, and that the street-car, now almost empty, was passing the gymnasium. At the next stop he got off at the same time as a well-dressed man who asked him how to get to the house where the Dean of Law lived, and Joseph thought for a moment; he knew the way quite well, but did not feel capable of explaining it; it was too complicated and he shook his head.

"You don't live here?" the man asked.

Again Joseph shook his head and the man went away. Why had he asked that? Why was he interested in whether Joseph lived there or not? He looked kindly, but he had asked that question.

Joseph followed the pavement leading to the gymnasium and suddenly wondered what the time was. He pulled out his watch, but it had stopped at six o'clock. He had forgotten to wind it up last night. Last night, at eleven o'clock in the evening, he had forgotten to wind up this watch which he now held in his palm and looked at as though he had never seen it before. But he could not stay there, he must walk on or go in somewhere to get warm. The brick wall of the gymnasium towered near him. But he could not go in the gymnasium, because the boys there were naked, exposed their bodies. A little further off he could see the cafeteria with its tall chimney; the smell of cooking floated through the air.

Retracing his steps, he went towards the country, but the roads were blocked by the snow and he had to come back to the University. The clock on the library began to strike and he counted. Only eleven o'clock. Once more he wondered what he was going to do. He had an English class at eleven, but there could be no question of his going.

"Why?"

This word, which he spoke aloud, sounded in his ears as though it had been said by someone else, and it astonished him. Why, indeed? Was everything in his life going to stop? Was he not to go on eating, talking, reading? Why was he there in the snow, under the gymnasium wall? He could find no answer to this question.

In any case he was going to skip the English class. People were always doing it at the University, but up to now Joseph had not missed a single class. Today he would go to the library and install himself in one of the recesses with a book; this would prevent his wasting time.

A few minutes later he was mounting the library steps and pushing open the heavy door, but at that moment the same odd question came into his mind again: Why? He suddenly felt as though behind all his actions there was this silent question. Why are you going up these steps? Why are you pushing open this door? He went in. The warmth of the large, round room was pleasant and he stood there for a few seconds, his face relaxing. Finally he took off his overcoat and looked for a table, but the best places were taken. Everywhere there were students reading, or snoozing, overcome by the warmth under the great dome. In the silence he heard the hissing of the radiators.

Joseph walked almost right round the library on tiptoe before he found a place behind a great pile of overcoats and scarves on a table. With a sigh of weariness he sank into an arm-chair. On the other side of the table a boy Joseph did not know was almost asleep, with his head sunk on his chest.

How comfortable it was! A delicious warmth flowed into his hands, his legs, all through his body. With his elbows on the arms of the chair, he linked his fingers over his stomach and looked curiously out of the window. Everything was hidden in snow. The tips of the magnolia leaves near the library could just be seen like black tongues. The little brick path had been cleared. Joseph had often heard it said that nothing ever changed at the University, but this morning, for the first time, he felt a sort of gratitude for everything that did not alter. Generations of young men had sat there in that corner and, like him, looked out at the little brick path. In the spring and autumn the wistaria hung all over the arch on the right. This morning the snow allowed only a few black and twisted branches to be seen, but there would be wistaria again. The snow would melt, but under the snow were all those dead leaves. . . . He pressed his fingers tightly together and, as he turned away his eyes, he caught sight of a big book open on the table, near the pile of coats. It was a volume of the Encyclopædia Britannica, which someone had been consulting. His glance fell on the name of Holberg. He began automatically to read the biography of this man, of whom he had never heard. He learnt that, with the exception of

Voltaire, Holberg was the most important writer of his time, but Joseph had never read Voltaire. Still, the fact was worth remembering. Why? That question again. He shrugged his shoulders. By leaning forward he could see the library clock. Already twenty past eleven. At noon he ought to go to the cafeteria again, as he had yesterday, but he would not go. He was as tired as if he had been walking all day, and, leaning his arms on the volume of the Encyclopædia, he let his head sink down and fell asleep.

Noon was striking as he awoke. Joseph rubbed his eyes and glanced furtively around. The student who had been there before had gone and his place was taken by little John Stuart, the shy boy who had been made drunk and taken into town. He and Joseph exchanged a smile, but Stuart at once looked down to his book. He looked so serious that Joseph could hardly credit what Killigrew had told him about that incredibly indecent scene. One might almost have taken him for a child, in spite of his studious-looking glasses. And he had smiled at Joseph. Because of this, for a few minutes the latter felt a confused joy which overcame all his uneasiness, and his own smile was long in disappearing.

A quarter of an hour later he noticed that many of the students were leaving the library and he went out too, rather regretfully, but perhaps it was better not to stay too long in one place. On the other hand, he did not know where to go. At the cafeteria they were probably wondering at his absence: the bad-tempered woman he had met first, the boys in aprons, the boy with black eyes to whom he had spoken . . . He shook his head, as though putting an end to a discussion, and went down the library steps. The path cleared in the snow led to the covered arcades, but why should he go there? Beyond the arcades there were only trails. One led to the building where the literature class was being held, the other was hardly visible, and went in the direction of the concert hall. He suddenly felt hemmed in by the snow. It seemed, indeed, to be forcing him towards the long avenue and the orange street-car which had taken him into town, but on no account would he go back into town. Elsewhere, however, the paths were blocked.

He was cold and was beginning to feel hungry. For the moment the best thing seemed to be to go on walking until he had come to a decision, and going round the library he went between two ramparts of snow towards the gymnasium. When he had reached the door of the dark-brick building he slowed his steps. Others could go in, no doubt, but not he. He would never cross the threshold of that building. He looked at the tall cafeteria chimney between the trees. Perhaps he should go on towards the long avenue, but once there what would he do? But he walked on in that direction, his hands in his pockets, his head sunk forward. Suddenly he stopped dead; someone had just whistled softly behind him.

XXIV

HE did not turn round and the whistle was repeated, a little louder this time. Several thoughts passed through Joseph's mind, and his heart seemed to stop beating. He could not run. Nor could he stay still. With an effort which involved his whole being he turned his head and at the end of the little path he saw Praileau.

He was wearing black gloves and a thick sweater of white wool which came right up to his ears and looked yellow against the snow. Like Joseph, he was bare-headed and his hair was blown by the wind. Without moving, he signed to Joseph to come nearer, but the latter hesitated. Then Praileau left the path and moved off in the snow, which came to his knees, turning round once and waving to Joseph to follow him. The young man obeyed.

They walked one behind the other between the trees, their legs encumbered by the snow, and after a few minutes they reached a wooded hill, which they began to climb in silence. Praileau walked without haste, his head erect and his ears as red as cherries. He seemed to know his ground, mounting obliquely and without faltering, but Joseph followed him with difficulty, stumbling as his overcoat got in his way, and he was panting.

A quarter of an hour later they were standing face to face, a few yards apart, in the middle of a snow-covered wood. Around them was such a silence that they could hear their own blood singing in their ears.

"I waited for you around noon near the cafeteria," Praileau said at last. "I had to see you."

Almost immediately he added: "We shall be quiet here."

Joseph did not reply. He had the curious impression that the words that reached him were cutting through the air as though it were ice. Praileau watched him with eyes at once serious and shining, his cheeks reddened by the cold, and he, too, was panting as he stood a little above Joseph, who raised his face towards him and said nothing.

"Why don't you say something?" Praileau asked. "You look like someone who has just done something stupid."

He let a few seconds go by, and faced by Joseph's silence went on: "I've made you come all the way here to help you. That seems odd to you, doesn't it? But you were always mistaken about me because of our quarrel last September near the pond."

Seeing that Joseph did not move, he came down to him, took off his gloves, which he put down at his feet, and picked up a handful of snow, rubbing it on the astonished boy's face.

"Wake up!" he cried. "You're like a sleepwalker on the edge of a roof. Get angry! I'd rather you were angry than gloomy. You're done for if you stay like that."

"What do you mean?" Joseph said, wiping his face with his sleeve.

Praileau put on his gloves.

"It's about Moira," he said. "No, don't move. You've got to listen. I knew she was going to your room. Everyone knew it, unfortunately. Everyone except your little . . . parson, who knows nothing."

Joseph made a movement, but Praileau seized his arm, as though to stop him running away.

"I tried to wreck this absurd scheme. I'm not your enemy, Joseph. But Moira had got it into her head she was going to see you and I knew it would end badly. Her friend Selina encouraged her. Selina has a room at Mrs. Dare's, belonging to a boy who's left the University.

When she saw that Moira hadn't come home this morning she went to Mrs. Ferguson around nine o'clock. They looked for Moira."

"They looked . . ." Joseph repeated.

"Yes, they looked for her and they didn't find her. Perhaps she ran away? Perhaps she was frightened . . . answer me!"

Joseph looked at Praileau and said nothing. Their eyes met and they were silent for some time. Then in a lower voice Praileau began to speak again.

"I hoped she had run away. What's so bad, you see, is that Selina lost her head and called the police. If, as I fear, something very serious happened last night you must not go back to your room, Joseph. There might be someone there who would ask you questions and a man who asks questions often has a pair of handcuffs in his pocket."

At these words Joseph went white and his mouth opened as though he were going to speak. A momentary flash of disdain appeared on Praileau's face and he lowered his eyes.

"I don't know what you were thinking of doing," he said, "but if you don't run away you might as well give yourself up tonight."

He waited, then asked: "Do you want me to help you get away?"

Joseph's hoarse voice asked after a pause: "Why do you want to help me?"

Praileau seemed taken aback by the question, but he recovered himself.

"That's my business," he said. "In any case, unless you're quite crazy you'll do what I tell you, because

227

they may quite well be looking for you already. Listen carefully. The wood we're in now runs for more than a mile above one of the roads out of town. If you go straight on in that direction you'll come to a gully. Are you paying attention?"

Joseph nodded.

"You'll wait in the wood until nightfall. Then you must go down the gully and on to the road. You'll wait there, for an hour if necessary. A car will go by and slow down, and then stop just by the gully to let you get in. This car will take you to the port of Norfolk. You'll be told what you have to do to get out of the country in a merchant ship. It'll be difficult. You'll need courage, daring and cunning, but it's your only chance. Do you accept?"

Joseph did not answer.

"There'll be two men in the car," Praileau went on. "I can vouch for them as for myself. You have nothing to fear."

He paused, then said more harshly: "You have my word of honour."

As he spoke he reddened.

"I don't see why you're doing this," Joseph muttered.

Praileau looked him up and down.

"I'm waiting for your answer," he said.

He was now only a few paces from Joseph, a little above him, and looked at him in silence. His colour was heightened by the cold to a bright red and seemed to make his eyes shine more strongly under his proudly curving eyebrows. Joseph lowered his eyes, in spite of himself, and could not help gazing at Praileau's hands in the black gloves, and for a reason he could not explain the black gloves made them look like an executioner's hands. He himself leant against a tree, his arms limp. Fatigue and misery had painted green shadows round his eyes and he breathed with difficulty.

"I accept," he said at last.

Praileau came nearer, visibly relieved.

"I'm going back to the University," he said in a softer voice. "In an hour's time I shall have made all the necessary arrangements. If you do what you're told you'll be safe. I'm sure of that, Joseph. Shall we shake hands? This time I'm asking you."

With a simultaneous gesture they took off their gloves and their hands met.

"Do you remember the evening we fought?" Joseph asked.

"Yes, of course."

"You said that one day I should know why you didn't want to speak to me."

Praileau lowered his eyes.

"It's too late now. Our paths will not cross again."

"I should like to know."

"I could never tell you."

Without abruptness he took away his hand and looked at Joseph for a long time.

"Good luck," he said in a muffled voice.

Joseph watched him put on his gloves and go away under the trees. After a minute Praileau had disappeared.

XXV

Joseph stood motionless for some time, then began to walk in the direction Praileau had pointed out. He walked slowly and in the deep silence of the wood heard only the murmur of his own breathing, but he soon caught the distant rumble of a snow-plough on the road, which could be seen through the trees. All around Joseph the light of the sun seemed caught in the sparkling whiteness, which threw it back at the sky, and he kept on putting his fists to his eyes with a little grimace of pain. After a moment he stopped to rest and then saw the snow-plough, which went by with a hollow growl, between two dazzling sheaves.

The noise consoled him; anything was better than the silence and, in the silence, the disturbing sound of his own breathing. He listened, following the big black machine in his imagination as it went away. Now he could no longer hear it. Shutting his eyes, he could see himself lying on a bed, as though on the cool snow, a bed like his own at home. Memories of childhood had been coming back to him all through the morning, in particular the memory of some slight illness which had kept him in his room for a week, that room whose smell he could recapture, the smell of board walls, mingled with the smell of the blanket which his mother pulled up round his neck to keep him warm.

Suddenly he wrenched himself away from the tree against which he was leaning and began walking again, this time in the opposite direction. He had only to walk in his own footmarks and these holes in the snow guided him, made his movements easier. They seemed to draw him on and he walked, almost asleep. At one point the trail divided and he recognised the spot Praileau had mentioned.

A few minutes later he was again passing the walls of the gymnasium, and he soon reached the great avenue. Then he began walking more quickly. Two or three hundred yards further on he was at the beginning of his street. It was about two o'clock and most of the students were in town. Those who saw him did not stop to speak, and he did not recognise any of them; he was almost running, but just before he reached Mrs. Ferguson's house caution made him stop. Praileau's warning rang in his ears suddenly like a cry of alarm: "Don't go back to your room!"

He hesitated a moment, then went up a narrow alley, which ran round the next house. This led to the waste land planted with bushes, which extended to the railway line; in spite of himself he looked for the place where he had dug the grave, but he could see nothing, nothing but the snow, over which the sun seemed to have thrown a web of fire.

His heart beat so fast that he had to stop to get his breath, then he stepped over the little wall and ran across the garden. When he was in front of David's window he took off one of his gloves and knocked on the window-pane. A little time went by and he felt he was about to drop with weariness when the window was raised and David's face appeared. Joseph opened his mouth, but no sound came out. Without a word David seized him by the shoulders and helped him climb into the room. Then he shut the window and went over to lock the door.

Joseph stood in the middle of the room, his knees trembling, supporting himself by one hand on the back of a chair, and he looked round, blinking, like a man dazed by exhaustion. Then he was conscious of being led towards the bed, where he fell, half-sitting, his legs dangling. At this moment, as through a mist, he saw David kneeling down to unlace his shoes, and he murmured: "Leave them, David, leave them."

But he was not capable of making a gesture to stop him, and after a moment the shoes fell on the floor and David took off Joseph's coat and forced him to lie down, throwing a blanket over him. Joseph turned his face to the wall and his hair shone on the white pillow.

"David, listen."

"Don't talk, sleep."

"If you knew . . ." Joseph went on in blurred tones.

"I want you to sleep. You can talk later."

There was a silence, then Joseph's voice was heard again, but this time each word was uttered with extraordinary distinctness in a hoarse whisper.

"I've killed Moira . . ."

He waited for a moment, then went on: "She's buried under the trees, on the other side of the little wall."

David did not move and said nothing, but a shadow passed over his face, which became ashy grey. With his hand on the head of the bed he stayed quite still and seemed to be holding his breath; his eyes did not leave Joseph's head, just visible above the blanket. At last he heard the sound of deep regular breathing. Joseph was asleep.

'That was why they came,' David thought.

Moving away from the bed, he put a chair in front of

the door, as though to guard the entrance, and sat down with his hands on his knees, looking at the form lying under the blanket. After some minutes he took a little Testament from his pocket and opened it at random, but he was trembling so much that the book slid out of his hands. Then, slipping to his knees, he tried to say a prayer, and collapsed, face downwards, on the floor, as though someone had pushed him by the shoulder.

When he got up at last his first care was to dip the corner of a towel in water and pass it over his face to wipe away the traces of tears; then he took his place by the door and waited. A ray of sunlight fell on the work-table and moved slowly across the room, as though pointing out one object after another: first the side of a book, then a rose in the wall-paper above the head of the sleeper, then a corner of the pillow:

Suddenly Joseph woke up.

"The car!" he cried.

David got up and went to him.

"You must have been dreaming," he said gently.

"Yes, I was dreaming," Joseph said, opening his eyes. "What time is it?" he asked.

"After four."

Joseph propped himself on his elbow.

"It will soon be dark," he said, as though speaking to himself.

Seizing David's hand he held it and raised child-like eyes to him.

"Why did it all happen?" he asked.

David shook his head.

"I don't know," he murmured. "God sometimes permits . . ."

233

"We won't mention God," Joseph said in a changed voice.

He let go of David's hand and got off the bed, sitting down on a chair to put on his shoes. Leaning over, he pulled the laces with an air of concentration and his hair fell over his eyes.

"In future," he said, lacing his shoes, "I shall keep all these things in my heart."

David came a little nearer and asked: "What are you going to do? There was someone in your room a short time ago. Then I saw someone in the street, near the house."

"I know what I have to do," Joseph said, putting on his overcoat. "I've had enough. I'll tell everything."

He turned to David and abruptly took him by the shoulders, and in a suddenly husky voice said: "David, you and I believe in the same things. You remember that Christ said we should not judge?"

"I don't judge you, I have never judged you," David burst out hurriedly, "I've always thought that you were better than I am. I still think so. I shall never be anything but a little clergyman. But you . . ."

The words stuck in his throat and he put one hand on Joseph's chest, as though this gesture would complete the sentence he was incapable of pronouncing.

"That's all right," said Joseph. "This evening you will go to see a student called Praileau. He lives in number 44 in the East Lawn. You'll tell him from me . . ."

"Yes, Joseph, I'm listening."

"You'll tell him simply that it wasn't possible."

"Will he understand?"

"He'll understand what I myself understand now."

They looked at each other, then Joseph opened the door and left the room.

He left the house without haste and crossed the garden to push open the little gate. Several people were passing in the street, but no one paid any attention to him, and he went along the pavement, which had been cleared, when suddenly he remembered Moira's letter. He opened his overcoat and took off a glove; it was still in his jacket pocket. If he liked he could tear it up or put it into the next mail box. He stopped to think, and decided to leave it where it was with its message, which was still unknown to him, but which was yet part of his destiny. Slowly he rebuttoned his overcoat.

The light wavered behind the trees, each branch showing white against the pale blue sky, now turning grey. The library clock rang out in the distance and in the dusk was heard the hard, fresh voice of a small boy calling an evening newspaper. With beating heart Joseph went on his way.

At the corner of the street a man came towards him.

THE END

QUARTET ENCOUNTERS

The purpose of this paperback series is to bring together influential and outstanding works of twentieth-century European literature in translation. Each title has an introduction by a distinguished contemporary writer, describing a personal or cultural 'encounter' with the text, as well as placing it within its literary and historical perspective.

Quartet Encounters will concentrate on fiction, although the overall emphasis is upon works of enduring literary merit, whether biography, travel, history or politics. The series will also preserve a balance between new and older works, between new translations and reprints of notable existing translations. Quartet Encounters provides a much-needed forum for prose translation, and makes accessible to a wide readership some of the more unjustly neglected classics of modern European literature.

Aharon Appelfeld · *The Retreat*

'A small masterpiece . . . the vision of a remarkable poet'
New York Times Book Review

Alain · *The Gods*

'There are not a few of us in the world who think Alain was, and remains, one of the greatest men of our time. I would not myself hesitate to say, the greatest'
André Maurois

Gaston Bachelard · *The Psychoanalysis of Fire*

'. . . he is a philosopher, with a professional training in
the sciences, who devoted most of the second phase of
his career to promoting that aspect of human nature
which often seems most inimical to science: the poetic
imagination . . .'
J.G. Weightman, *The New York Review of Books*

Robert Bresson · *Notes on the Cinematographer*

'[Bresson] is the French cinema, as Dostoyevsky
is the Russian novel and Mozart is German music'
Jean-Luc Godard, *Cahiers du Cinéma*

Hermann Broch · *The Sleepwalkers*

'One of the greatest European novels . . .
masterful' Milan Kundera

E.M. Cioran · *The Temptation to Exist*

'Cioran is one of the most delicate minds of real power
writing today. Nuance, irony, and refinement are the
essence of his thinking . . .' Susan Sontag

René Crevel · *Babylon*

'He was born a rebel the way others are born with blue
eyes' Philippe Soupault

Stig Dagerman · *The Games of Night*

'One is haunted by a secret and uneasy suspicion
that [Dagerman's] private vision, like Strindberg's
and Kafka's, may in fact be nearer the truth of things
than those visions of the great humanists, such as
Tolstoy and Balzac, which people call universal'
Michael Meyer

Stig Dagerman · *German Autumn*

'[*German Autumn*] attracted, and still deserves,
attention, partly because [Dagerman] had a sharp eye
for
concrete details, partly because he could argue
pungently, but mainly because he dared to see German
individuals as suffering human beings rather than
simply
as tokens of national disgrace or guilt' Robin Fulton

Grazia Deledda · *After the Divorce*

'What [Deledda] does is create the passionate complex
of a primitive populace' D.H. Lawrence

Marcellus Emants · *A Posthumous Confession*

'Since the time of Rousseau we have seen the growth
of the genre of the *confessional novel*, of which
A Posthumous Confession is a singularly pure
example.
Termeer [the narrator), claiming to be unable to keep
his dreadful secret, records his confession and leaves it
behind as a monument to himself, thereby turning a
worthless life into art' J.M. Coetzee

Carlo Emilio Gadda · *That Awful Mess on Via Merulana*

'One of the greatest and most original Italian novels
of our time' Alberto Moravia

Andrea Giovene · *Sansevero*

'Some novels can be flirted with, others constitute a brief
affair. Occasionally one is lured into a long marriage,
when the early tensions and subsequent *longueurs*
stabilize at last into a solid relationship. So it is reading
The Book of Giuliano Sansevero. One can see why, on
its way to this country . . . its author has been
compared with Proust and Lampedusa' *Daily Telegraph*

Julien Green · *Moira*

'Green's technique is Victorian-Gothic – his novels are highly melodramatic – but he is a modernist because his subject is the Nietzschean one of "man without God" '
Martin Seymour-Smith

Martin A. Hansen · *The Liar*

'[*The Liar*] is both a vindication of religious truth and a farewell to the traditional modes of extended fiction. It is haunted by literary ghosts, and English readers will recognize the shadowy forms of Hans Anderson . . . and Søren Kierkegaard' Eric Christiansen

Eugene Ionesco · *Fragments of a Journal*

'I am not too sure whether I am dreaming or remembering, whether I have lived or dreamt it. Memories quite as much as dreams arouse in me the strongest feelings of the unreality and the ephemerality of the world . . .'
Eugene Ionesco, *Present Past, Past Present*

Gustav Janouch · *Conversations with Kafka*

'I read it and was stunned by the wealth of new material . . . which plainly and unmistakably bore the stamp of Kafka's genius' Max Brod

Ismaïl Kadaré · *The General of the Dead Army*

'Ismaïl Kadaré is presenting his readers not merely with a novel of world stature — which is already a great deal — but also, and even more important, with a novel that is the voice of ancient Albania herself, speaking to today's world of her rebirth' Robert Escarpit

Miroslav Krleža · *On the Edge of Reason*

'Paris had its Balzac and Zola; Dublin, its Joyce;
Croatia, its Krleža . . . one of the most accomplished,
profound authors in European literature . . .'
Saturday Review

Pär Lagerkvist · *The Dwarf*

'A considerable imaginative feat'
Times Literary Supplement

Valery Larbaud · *Fermina Marquez*

'As a psychological study of male adolescence it is
delicate, touching, unsentimental; the atmosphere of the
school is evoked with an unforgettable nostalgic
vivacity' Francis Wyndham

Osip Mandelstam · *The Noise of Time*

'Clarence Brown's translation of Mandelstam not only
gives English readers the greatest twentieth-century
stylist in Russian but is also one of the finest examples
ever of the translator's art: a miracle of accuracy, tone
and feeling of period' Guy Davenport

Henry de Montherlant · *The Bachelors*

'One of those carefully framed, precise and acid
studies on a small canvas in which French writers
again and again excel' V.S. Pritchett

Stratis Myrivilis · *Life in the Tomb*

'*Life in the Tomb* has moments of great literary beauty
and of more than one kind of literary power. In 1917,
Myrivilis was twenty-five. "Before I entered the trenches
I had not the slightest inkling of life's true worth.
From now on, however, I shall savour its moments one
by one . . ." ' Peter Levi

Pier Paolo Pasolini · *A Dream of Something*

'. . . indisputably the most remarkable figure to have emerged in Italian arts and letters since the Second World War' Susan Sontag

Luigi Pirandello · *Short Stories*

'The outer world of Pirandello's stories – the appearance of its reality – has a deceptive monotony and a deceptive variety. The monotony is the mask which society exacts from us; the variety is the pathetic series of fragmentary masks in which we strut about the world' Frederick May

D.R. Popescu · *The Royal Hunt*

'Popescu's style may be compared to that of Gabriel García Márquez in *One Hundred Years of Solitude*, although it is more concrete and somewhat sharper . . .' J.E. Cottrell and M. Bogdan

Rainer Maria Rilke · *Rodin and other Prose Pieces*

'[Rilke's] essay remains the outstanding interpretation of Rodin's œuvre, anticipating and rendering otiose almost all subsequent criticism' William Tucker, *The Language of Sculpture*

Rainer Maria Rilke · *Selected Letters 1902–1926*

'By will-power and concentration, a sense of which is immanent in all his letters, as if some great quiet animal were crouching there, Rilke made himself into a great European genius, probably the last of the breed' John Bayley

Lou Andreas-Salomé · *The Freud Journal*

'Lou Andreas-Salomé was a woman with a remarkable
flair for great men and . . . it was said of her that she had
attached herself to the greatest men of the nineteenth
and twentieth centuries Nietzsche and Freud
respectively'
Ernest Jones, *The Life and Work of Sigmund Freud*

Boris Vian · *Froth on the Daydream*

'The greatest love novel of our time' Raymond Queneau

Elio Vittorini · *Conversation in Sicily*

'One puts down this novel feeling that one has had an
experience as valid as life and as art' Stephen Spender

Stanislaw Ignacy Witkiewicz · *Insatiability*

'A study of decay: mad, dissonant music, erotic
perversion, . . . and complex psychopathic personalities'
Czeslaw Milosz